SUSAN VAUGHAN

D1521876

NEVER
SURRENDER

TASK
FORCE
EAGLE

Published by Gullwood Press
Copyright 2013 Susan Hofstetter Vaughan
Cover design by www.formatting4U.com

ISBN: 1489560289
ISBN-13: 978-1489560285

PRAISE FOR SUSAN VAUGHAN'S BOOKS

"NEVER SURRENDER is the first book in author Susan Vaughan's new series and now I can't wait for the rest of the books to be released. This is a fast paced romantic suspense with a yummy hero and an independent heroine." – Reader Sheila S - 5 stars on Amazon.com.

"NEVER SURRENDER is filled with action, suspense, romance and a number of sneaky little twists and turns. I very much enjoy when an author lets you play along with solving the mystery by feeding you little bits and pieces." – Fresh Fiction

"Susan Vaughan writes an intensely romantic thriller.... This is an excellent tale of people at their best and worst learning to work together through adversity." - The Romance Studio about PRIMAL OBSESSION

"ONCE BURNED is action packed, with a number of twists and turns that will keep the reader guessing and reading. This...is an excellent action romance series." --Fresh Fiction

ALSO BY SUSAN VAUGHAN

DEDICATION

For all the writers who've guided and advised me about this book, and especially for my friends and critters, who made this book sing: Luanna Nau, Debora Noone, Judi Phillips. You all are the best.

ACKNOWLEDGMENTS

Many thanks to the writers and law enforcement experts of Crime Scene Writers for your help with many issues in this book

..

TASK FORCE EAGLE
Protecting their country and the women they love

A Romantic Suspense Trilogy

When federal agents Rick Cruz, Jake Wescott, and
Holt Donovan go after a Mexican cartel kingpin,
they face unexpected hazards—to their hearts.

NEVER SURRENDER
ONCE BURNED
TWICE A TARGET

- 1 -

Ricardo Cruz shook his head. Shit, another dead end. "That's it. The bird has flown."

He and the other Task Force Eagle agents had driven three hours from Boston to Portland, Maine, *por nada*. He unzipped his raid jacket and placed his SIG-Sauer P239 in the holster.

Holt Donovan turned his DEA cap around backward, the lid a switch from his usual cowboy hat. "Our quarry's beat-up Ford Focus is still parked out in the snow. Abandoning his wheels looks odd."

"Search warrants won't be good after today," ATF Agent Jake Wescott said, his Maine drawl softening his downer message.

"Good point." Rick directed the others to re-interview the landlord and question the other tenants while he searched the suspect's apartment.

Upstairs, he shot the deadbolt behind him and frowned at the dingy one-room garret euphemistically termed a studio. He wouldn't need long. Someone had beaten him to the search.

Whatever the dump contained lay in the middle of the floor.

Stuffing from the cheap futon mattress was scattered around like dirty clumps of the snow outside. Unmatched flatware and utensils formed a tangled heap on the grimy linoleum. Yesterday's *Portland Press Herald* rested undisturbed on the stained coffee table.

Aside from the clumsy toss, the place resembled a college dorm room more than a drug smuggler's digs. Rock posters tacked to the walls. Beer bottles and peanut butter jars alternated on the one set of dusty shelves.

Jordan Paris might have gotten caught up in the drug operation without knowing the score until it was too late.

Hands shielded with latex gloves, Rick picked up the newspaper. The front page had his boss announcing the indictment of two Mexicans captured last month.

Two little fish. With one dead exception, the big ones had gotten clean away. Leaving them with a minnow, the Paris kid.

"*Mierda.*" Rick tossed down the paper.

He looked around a few more minutes. Worthless. He'd learn little until the fingerprint report. Wescott and Donovan must have finished downstairs. He switched off the light, and March's early darkness drenched the small room. The stairway below creaked.

He sucked in a breath. Adrenaline surged. He flattened himself against the wall behind the door.

Three knocks rattled the apartment's thin paneled door. He waited. If it was Wescott or

Donovan, they'd call his name. He held his breath and gripped his nine millimeter.

The doorknob jiggled. A key clinked in the lock. Then the knob turned, and the door eased open.

In the spill of light into the room, he saw a gloved hand at the door's edge. A hand holding a small automatic.

Before the intruder could make a move, Rick knocked away the pistol.

A sharp gasp of shock and surprise. Then the intruder slammed his chest with something hard, knocking the breath from his lungs. Before he recovered enough to get a good hold, the smaller man swung a kick.

Letting his thigh take the blow, Rick flipped his attacker and slammed on top of him. Darkness prevented a clear look. He jabbed his gun barrel at the guy's throat. "Federal agent. Give it up, and you won't get hurt."

The intruder cocked his head in a careful nod.

Easing off his captive, Rick reached inside the unzipped coat to pat down for weapons. A wool sweater covered a slight torso with curves and soft, round . . . breasts.

What the hell?

As he lifted his gun from her throat and sat back on his heels, the woman dragged in a deep breath. "You . . . you," she gasped, "Nazi bully. This is what I pay taxes for? To be crushed and then groped?"

At her outburst, his lips twitched with a smile. The kid's girlfriend? An accomplice? She sounded irate, but not street tough. He kept his gun on her and flicked the light switch.

In the glare of the bare overhead bulb, the

woman blinked. She had a turned-up nose and wide mouth, lips clamped in displeasure. Her eyes shot green fire at him.

He leaned across her to retrieve her gun, but found instead a more innocuous item. Chagrinned, he handed her the small flashlight.

Beside the woman lay a voluminous purse. Her ramming weapon.

He quickly checked the contents. Wallet, zippered day planner, hairbrush, and various other female junk, but no weapons other than the leaden bag. "I expected to see bricks inside."

"I wish." Her chin shot up a notch. It was gently pointed, emphasizing the heart shape of her face.

"You can get up now." Rising, he offered her a hand. "Who are you?"

Refusing his help, she scooted backward before leaping to her feet in an agile motion. Reddish curls threatened to spring free of a carnivorous-toothed clip. Little butterfly earrings dangled from her earlobes. "First I want to see ID. You have a badge, don't you?"

He tucked away his gun and refrained from pointing out the word *POLICE* on his raid jacket. "Yes, ma'am, Special Agent Ricardo Cruz of the U. S. Drug Enforcement Administration." He held up his ID case.

Juliana Paris's racing heart gradually slowed to a jog. Gathering poise, she took her time studying the official card. DEA? For all his self-absorption and impulsiveness, Jordan was a straight arrow about drugs. It made no sense.

The agent regarded her with professional suspicion. Mocking her efforts at cool control, her cheeks burned under the scrutiny. She made a production of stashing the flashlight, cracked and probably useless, in her bag.

"I suppose you're who you say you are, but what are you doing in my brother's apartment—in the dark?" Straightening to her full five-foot-three, she folded her arms.

"Your brother." The DEA agent rubbed his knuckles on his jaw. "Can you prove that Jordan Paris is your brother?"

She would not be reduced to jelly by a good-looking man with a sexy voice. "Prove? Not really." She rummaged in her bag. "But here's my driver's license."

Agent Cruz didn't take the license from her, but framed the hand holding it with his own. "Portsmouth, New Hampshire? You drove here this afternoon?"

She nodded.

He continued to grip her hand. His tanned fingers contrasted starkly with her pale redhead's skin. When he released her, she snatched back her hand as if from a flame.

"Why the flashlight?"

"Sometimes Jordan forgets to pay his electricity bills. My brother has issues but he's no criminal." For the first time, the condition of the room registered. Everything strewn around. One hand flew to her throat. "What's going on? What have you done?"

"First explain why you're here and what you know about Jordan's recent activities." He gestured for her to take a seat.

Until he sat, she would stand. She wasn't about

to have him looming over her. "I'm not sure what Jordan's been up to lately. That's sort of why I came."

"You must know where he works." His gaze concealed whether he knew the answer.

"Until two months ago, he worked for Vinson Seafood on a dragger. When the boat went in for repairs, he was laid off. He's been out of work since."

Juliana wished he wouldn't keep looking at her with such concentrated focus. It was unnerving. She licked her lower lip.

As if too warm, the agent threw off his windbreaker. His black flak vest emblazoned with the yellow letters DEA confirmed his status. His black turtleneck and pants displayed a trim yet powerful build. With a cape, this man would make a better Zorro than that Spanish actor. No, she wouldn't think of him that way. She blinked away the image.

Cruz sat on the futon across the room. "So what prompted your visit today?"

Perching on the edge of a metal folding chair, she decided to tell the truth. Mostly. "He phoned me this morning and said he'd gotten mixed up in something. He was afraid."

She'd just returned after her morning jog and didn't have the breath to argue with him. His words came back to her. *"Jules, I'm in over my head. I gotta disappear. Meet me, and I'll tell you everything."* But now . . . She linked her fingers tightly in her lap.

"What else did he tell you?" Cruz scrawled in a pocket-size notebook.

"He only asked me to come here. I'm sure he's

not involved with drugs. Where is he?"

"I hoped you could tell me. I came to interview your brother, but he's not here."

Mouth tight, she gestured at the room's condition. "And you did *this*? Did you suspect he was hiding in the sofa cushions? Maybe in a drawer?"

His half-grin indented a dimple. "I found this place exactly as you see it. I had just looked around and doused the lights when you arrived. I do have a search warrant."

A search warrant. What was Jordan mixed up in?

Cruz opened a package of mints and offered it to her. When she refused, he popped one in his mouth. "I quit smoking a year ago, but now I'm addicted to peppermint."

"I wouldn't know." No way would she think of this agent in a personal way or be suckered by his little-boy grin. "What do you think Jordan has done?"

"For the last month, he's driven a truck for Sudsy's Seafood from Cumberland Harbor to Boston and Hartford. Hidden among the lobsters and clams were containers of heroin and cocaine, smuggled in from offshore to Dwight Pettit, a.k.a. Sudsy."

Jordan had fallen into quicksand. She rubbed at her belly, aching as if some creature were gnawing at her. "What makes you think he knew what was in the truck?"

Cruz's broad shoulders lifted in a shrug. "We have only circumstantial evidence, but he's our best hope of catching the drug gang. Sudsy has disappeared."

"Disappeared. And now so has Jordan?" Talons pierced her. She chewed her bottom lip. *Jordan, somehow I've failed you.* "But his car is still here."

"He packed up. Landlord saw him leave with a duffel." He jerked a thumb toward the bottles and the posters. "Other than his art collection, he didn't leave much behind."

"He doesn't have much. Mostly he lives on a fishing boat."

"Will you help me find him?"

The last thing she'd do. She shot to her feet and gathered her parka around her. "I wish you luck in catching the drug dealers, but I have no idea where my brother went." Slinging her bag onto one shoulder, she started to the door.

He stepped in front of her. "It's in his best interest for you to help me find him."

She forced herself to meet his gaze. Sooty lashes framed his dark eyes. His warm breath smelled of peppermint. But this man wanted only to solve his case. He didn't care about Jordan or his problems.

"I can't help you, Agent Cruz. I don't know where Jordan might be. Please move."

He handed her a notepad and a pen. "You're free to go once you write down your address and phone number."

She printed her information and handed the items back. "You'll contact me if you find Jordan?"

He stepped aside and opened the door. "You can clean up if you like once we're finished. I'll let you know."

"Fine." She marched through the open door and down the narrow stair. Though he made scarcely a sound, she sensed Cruz behind her. Feathery wings fluttered in her stomach.

Three flights down, they reached the small, dim foyer. The entry smelled of tobacco and rancid grease and worse. Wherever Jordan hid, she hoped it was cleaner than this dump.

"Jordan may have cause to thank you for helping *us* find him first," Cruz said softly.

Whirling, she shot him a glare. "What do you mean?"

"Two thugs who don't care about Miranda rights or asking first before shooting were looking for your baby brother last night. Maybe he came home and found the place tossed. We think that's why he high-tailed it. If they want him bad, they could come looking for *you* too."

Her breath stuttered.

"I know too much, Jules. I'm in over my head."

If he was in danger, maybe . . . no, if Jordan was mixed up in this drug trafficking, she had to protect him. From all sides, including the DEA. She wouldn't let what happened to their dad happen to Jordan. Whatever it took. "I'll encourage my brother to turn himself in, but I won't betray him. Now, am I free to go?"

Stiffly, his eyes as hard as obsidian, Cruz bent his head in a courtly bow rather than a nod. This Zorro knew when to yield and sheathe his sword.

After the front door closed behind her, Juliana heard a muffled thud. Had the controlled, charming Agent Cruz slammed his fist into the wall?

- 2 -

Rick gripped his throbbing knuckles. *Ay, idiota*, he blew that one big time. His usual techniques that charmed every other female failed with the delectable Juliana Paris. Courage and loyalty, even if the brother didn't deserve it.

He popped another mint as Jake Wescott entered the hallway. He tucked his aching fist behind his back. "Hope you had better luck than I did."

Wescott thumbed his ball cap higher on his head. "We have a saying in Maine. Which is better, no luck or bad luck?"

Rick described his visit to the apartment. He slid his police radio from his windbreaker and advised the Portland agents stationed behind the building they could return to headquarters.

"Now what?'

"Got a hot date in Boston. Don't want to be late."

"Who's your babe of the week?" Wescott asked.

He grinned. "And have you poach? Forget it,

Jake." His date was with the case files, but he had a reputation to uphold. No settling into being a drudge. He'd keep his carefree way of life as long as possible. How could he choose just one when the menu offered too many luscious flavors and varieties? Like his suspect's feisty sister. The notion stopped him cold.

Inhaling the frigid air, he swept a glance down the street. Even this pleasant small city had run-down sections. The smudgy dusk lent this one an even seedier appearance. But he saw no suspicious vehicles and no loiterers. He and Wescott hurried toward their sedan where Donovan awaited them.

"If only El Águila and his man Olívas had been sitting in Sudsy Pettit's kitchen," Rick said, "we could've wound up this whole damn case." And put an end to the gang that had killed his brother.

"There'd only be another to take his place. Keeps us in business."

"Are we jinxed or what?"

"Maybe voodoo."

"No fair picking on my Cuban heritage," Rick said. "Watch out, or a Santero priest will put a dead chicken in your bed."

"Who cares, hot shot? I never get to sleep there." Wescott sighed. "The landlord did give me detailed descriptions of those two heavies who were here last night."

"See? All is not lost. And we have another lead. Jordan Paris's sister." Rick grinned, anticipating the challenge.

"From what you said, she wasn't impressed with you. Has the famous Cruz charm met an immovable object?"

"I didn't grow up with four sisters for nothing. She won't be able to resist me a second time." She was hiding something, for damn sure. And he needed what she knew.

Juliana tossed her backpack on the sofa. She scrubbed at her gritty eyes. "Jordan, you poor, gullible kid, what have you gotten mixed up in?"

The hour was late and she was tired, but she had to figure out what to do. Dammit, he'd sucked her into his mess, one more dangerous than his usual tangles. Talons clawed her stomach again. She twisted a finger in her hair and chewed her bottom lip.

"Mrrr," came a plaintive voice from the kitchen alcove.

"Yes, yes, Speedy, I know—dinner time." She kicked off her boots and hurried to do the cat's bidding.

From his perch on the kitchenette bar, the raccoon-brown feline replied his assent and twitched his tail.

Juliana opened a can of liver and mixed it with dry food. "Come on down, sweetie. Din-din's ready." She set the meal down beside his water dish. When the cat sniffed, she lifted the blue bowl to the counter. "What *was* I thinking? Here, your highness."

With a murmur she took as thank you, the animal tucked into his meal at a pace appropriate to his name.

After pouring water and measuring coffee, she started the brewing. And mulling. Jordan's vow to stand on his own feet and on his own bank account had blown away with the March wind. She withdrew a yellow lined notepad from a drawer and listed places her brother might hide—three or four friends, Uncle Grady, camp.

His meal completed, Speedy sat up to wash his whiskers. He cast a skeptical amber eye on his mistress.

"I know. Jordan has gone too far this time. But I practically raised him, and . . ." Oh, where could he be? Was he safe? She swallowed more questions about the danger he'd landed in and dumped the cat's bowl in the sink.

The light rap at the door startled her. *No, no, go away.* Before her drive to and from Portland, she'd spent spring break working five days at five different companies for Temps-R-Us, and her accounting assignment was due next week. She trudged to the door.

She checked the peephole. Venice Aaron. She adored her neighbor, but Venice had a knack of ferreting out her intimate secrets. She couldn't hide from her. Juliana pasted on a smile before undoing the locks.

"I brought you some library printouts. Thought you could use them for that humongous assignment we have." Venice was six feet tall and the color of coffee ice cream but friendly and warm as melted toffee. She held out a Macy's shopping bag.

Juliana accepted the bag. "Thanks. I owe you one. I do need to get my printer fixed."

"Finally got that number crunching behind me. Much more of this, and Venice is gonna need glasses on her big browns."

Juliana laughed. "You make enough money sewing for the theater department to pay for contact lenses."

"Got to look to the future, girlfriend. I want my own costume business." Venice swept into the living room, the long, knit, rose-colored tube of a dress embracing her statuesque body like shrink-wrap. "I cooked up this number for next week's one-act."

"Gorgeous, as usual." Juliana followed in her wake. "Coffee should be ready."

"Maybe half a cup, hon. I'm headed to campus in a few with some outfits for the kids to try on." Venice sleeked a hand from Speedy's head to his fluffy tail. "And how's my favorite kitty, hmmm?"

Juliana poured two mugs of coffee. Her mind slipped back to Jordan's words: *"I gotta disappear."* A headache throbbed behind her eyes.

"You're worried about something, and I'll bet it's not accounting." Venice blew on the hot brew. "Either your mother or Jordan. What's one of them done now?"

"I might as well tell you. You'd worm it out of me anyway." Juliana recited her truncated phone conversation with her brother and the results of her trip to Portland. She didn't mention the agent's warning.

"The DEA? Whoa, that's some serious shit." Venice said. "You got ideas about where Jordan might be hiding his fool self?"

"One or two. I want to find him first. I want to hear his side of it." And to make sure he was safe. She couldn't trust Agent Cruz or any cop. No way she'd trust the DEA to protect her baby brother.

Between classes and work, she would find the time. *Somehow.*

"Why not let the cops do the dirty work? Seems to me you take on too much responsibility for your family." Venice clucked her tongue.

She folded her arms. "And thank heavens one member of the Paris family acts like a grown-up. My naïve brother chases every hare-brained scheme that promises money, and Molly latches onto every paradise-promising, lame-brained man who takes hers."

"I understand, hon, but you can't be everybody's mom." Venice slid off the stool and smoothed her knit dress. She glided to the door. "I hope you know what you're doing, but that boy might be in danger. A big, strong government agent would come in handy."

When her friend left, Juliana picked up Speedy and nuzzled the fur between his ears. The cat rumbled a deep, rolling purr. She carried him to the window and stared out, picturing the DEA agent. Six-foot-plus, lean frame, hair and eyes as black as the starry sky above. "No way. If I never see Ricardo Cruz again, I'll be safer all around."

She released the cat, who muttered what might have been a cynical harrumph.

Below, a van with no headlights rolled from the street to the parking lot's edge. If it hadn't passed beneath a light, she wouldn't have seen it.

The agent's words echoed in her brain: *"They could come looking for you too."*

Juliana sank down beneath the window. Heart pounding like a tom-tom, she hugged her knees.

- 3 -

Two days later, Rick had found no trace of Jordan Paris. He logged off his computer and rubbed his knuckles, still tender from the right he'd given that door jamb. "Dammit!"

"What's the matter, Cruz? Can't decide which babe tonight?" Jake Wescott called across the big office the task force shared.

"Nah, he's bummed about the one female he couldn't rope with his charm," Holt Donovan added. He thumbed up the brim of his Stetson and leaned back in his swivel chair.

"You got it, Holt. Can't find Jordan Paris and can't get it on with his sister. Finally, for one smart woman, he really is the Invisible Man." Wescott hooted at his own joke.

Rick's stealth on SEAL missions had earned him the nickname. He grinned. "Go ahead and have your fun. How much of this case have you cracked while I've been trying to talk to Ms. Paris?"

Donovan coughed and removed the hat. "You

got me there. Her brother has plumb disappeared."

"Right." Rick's grin faded as he ticked off their progress on his fingers. "Only his fingerprints and the sister's in his apartment. No leads there. We impounded his car, so he has no wheels. No charges to his two credit cards, no plane tickets reserved, no checks cashed."

"If he's as reckless and gullible as his sister implied, why hasn't he made a mistake by now?" Wescott asked.

"Maybe he did. And the gang silenced him. For good." Rick's comment silenced the hilarity. Everyone began to pore over files.

He picked up the one he'd begun on Juliana Paris. Part-time temp worker, part-time student. Jordan was her only close relative except a mother, whereabouts unknown. Father deceased. No police record, no traffic tickets, small bank account. Her silent act looked bad for her and for her brother, but the lady checked out squeaky clean.

But why did she distrust the DEA enough to endanger herself and her brother? A search of the father came up with no prison record. Not even a traffic ticket. Nada.

Stymied, he slapped down the folder and considered Sudsy Pettit. How had he gotten away? The task force had kept their presence secret, not to spook the guy. Units had watched the harbor to ensure Pettit didn't escape in his boat or the refrigerated fish truck. Their pigeon had flown, but not before cleaning out his coop. No fingerprints. No personal items. No computer files. Only a pair of crutches left in a closet.

Another question oozed greasily in his gut. How

had so many busts gone sour and ops blown? It was as if the suspect had been warned.

He wouldn't allow the gang to slip the net. Snaring Carlos Olívas and the other assholes running the northeastern smuggling would save a hell of a lot of kids like his brother. If he could nail the head honcho El Águila himself, he might feel whole again. Rick curled his hands into fists. He refused to fail at shutting him down. Leak or no leak.

Juliana Paris was his only lead to her brother and the smugglers. He had to persuade her to cooperate.

Juliana leaned against her car door, her pen poised over her day planner, a low-tech loose-leaf binder instead of the digital one she couldn't afford. The same neighborhood of row houses that contained Jordan's apartment housed a number of his fellow fishermen and buddies. Not dangerous, just neglected in the way of temporary housing for people down on their luck. Or goalless, like Jordan, on the way to nowhere. Smells of fried food and uncollected garbage hung in the air.

She'd spent the past two days trying to track down anyone her brother might have confided in, anyone who might have a clue to where he had gone to hide. And came up empty.

He should've called her again. Wouldn't he know she'd worry? As if a lead ball weighed her stomach, a sharp pang tightened her muscles. She closed her eyes and tried to breathe evenly. She had to be strong and keep trying. Jordan's life might be at stake.

"Whooee, what a hunk!" said a girlish voice.

Juliana glanced up at the teenage girls sunning on the row-house step before her. This warm blue March day must've tempted a boy to hang out on the other side of the street. Oh, for life to be that simple.

"Arlene, let's take a little walk. I want a closer look at Tall, Dark, and Devastating." The girl, in low-hanging jeans and a clingy aqua belly shirt, sashayed down the steps.

"After that last dork, Missy, you said you were through with men," Arlene teased. "Besides he's too old for you."

"A hottie like him would tempt a nun, and window shopping doesn't mean you're gonna buy. Mm-mmm! Look at those broad shoulders in that fine leather jacket."

Reflecting on how to contact Jordan's old girlfriend, Juliana didn't search out the target of their admiration. Finally their words sparked a brain synapse.

Broad shoulders. Tall, Dark, and Devastating. Her pulse flip-flopped, and heat invaded her cheeks. Before she turned, she knew who the hunk was and who he waited for.

"Ms. Paris." With fluid masculine grace, Ricardo Cruz unfolded his long frame from the small stoop and doffed his mirrored sunglasses. His dark eyes skimmed her with warm appreciation as he crossed the narrow street.

"Agent Cruz. What are you doing here?" She dropped her planner beside her backpack on the passenger seat. She dug her fingernails into her palms against the power of his smile.

To one side, the two teenagers waited, mesmerized. They gaped at the agent as though he were handing out free concert tickets.

Observing the bulge of what was probably a pistol beneath his left arm, Juliana stiffened. She cast a glare at the two girls. They huffed in defeat and flounced away.

Agent Cruz slipped his sunglasses in an inner pocket. His intense regard threaded heat through her. The full impact of his attention made her the only woman in existence.

A deliberate male tactic. She gave herself a mental shake. "What do you want?"

"Merely to talk. How about lunch?"

"Sorry, I'm busy."

Cruz made a slight bow. The image of Zorro flashed in her mind. "A good detective takes care of herself. If you're hungry or cold, you can't do your job."

"Detective? Hardly." She shook her head. "I'm fine and I don't want to talk to you."

He examined a page in his pocket notepad. "This morning you've looped all over the city. Talked to four of Jordan's buddies before this one. Palmieri, is it? You need a break."

She zipped the planner in her backpack and slung the pack on with so much force she nearly lost her balance. "You've been following me. How dare you!"

"Protecting you, Ms. Paris. Protecting you." He shrugged. "Better me following you than El Águila's goons."

"El Águila? Who's that? No one's following me but you."

His dark eyes glimmered with suspicion. "Did they already contact you? Have you seen a tail?"

Her stomach prickled. *The van in the parking lot. Then this morning . . .* "Certainly not." She managed to keep her gaze steady, but she'd paused a second too long.

"I see." Perception glinted in his eyes. "Lunch and I'll give you the scoop on El Águila."

She shouldn't trust him but she had to know. "All right. There's a small sandwich shop a few blocks over on Congress Street. We can walk."

Ten minutes later, Rick sat across from Juliana and facing the entrance in a back booth at Sammy's Subs Plus. He could observe every table and booth. College pennants papered the walls. Tables, chairs, and booths gleamed with the USM blue and white. Except for them and a gray-haired couple, only fresh-faced students filled the seats.

Boys with shaved heads and torn jeans. Others in preppy collars and khakis. Girls in mere scraps of cloth or skirts that swept their ankles. International students—one in Middle Eastern headgear and a few Asians. No Hispanics. Not that El Águila's flunkies had to be Mexican or even look Hispanic. But no one here paid Juliana and him any undue attention.

"Order first." He picked up a menu from the table. "Then we'll talk."

"You're not buying me lunch. I'll pay for my own food." She speared him with a glare. "I came with you only because I want to know about this El Águila."

21

"Up to you." Rick observed her while she pretended to study the menu. She'd bound that glorious hair into a ponytail. He'd like to see it free around her shoulders.

He had to tread carefully. His cop's instinct also told him that Olívas posed an imminent threat to her. The idea of her brother caught in El Águila's talons reminded him of Rudy, but he wouldn't examine it too closely.

Removal of her jacket revealed a tiny butterfly tattoo on her neck. She wore layers of silky tops over her slim jeans. Simple but sexy. Damn, he had to curb his attraction. Sister of a suspected drug trafficker, she should interest him only as a lead.

Once they'd ordered, she said, "I haven't heard from my brother, if that's what you want to know. No e-mail, no text, no phone call, nothing."

"You must be very worried, Juliana."

The corners of her mouth trembled. "I have every right to be."

Since she allowed him to use her first name, he relaxed. Maybe it'd be okay. She'd talk to him. "Tell me about your brother. Jordan must be a special guy to merit such loyalty. I wonder if any of my sisters would stand up for me like that."

"Sisters? How many?" She closed her mouth as if regretting the personal question.

"Four. I'm in the middle, and to hear them tell it, the bane of their existence when we were growing up." He folded his hands on the table. "But we were talking about Jordan."

Her gaze slid to the tabletop, then to the throng around them. He could almost read her thoughts through her animated features and transparent coloring. He imagined her agile mind analyzing the pros and cons of sharing family information with him. Fascinating.

A quartet with physics texts exited the booth behind Juliana. They had eaten hunched over a laptop and some papers one of them juggled into a folder.

The waitress returned with their drinks, and Juliana peeled the paper from her straw with undue concentration. When she again regarded him, it was clear she'd answer questions, but would pounce on any misstep.

"My dad died when I was fifteen and Jordan was five. Molly—my mom—wasn't home much after that. She had to work two jobs."

"So responsibility for your brother fell to you?" She was more a parent to the kid than a sister. That explained her desperate concern.

She shrugged. "I went to parent conferences and helped him learn to read. Jordan struggled in school. He skipped a lot to hang out at the co-ops and talk to the fishermen. Some took him out on their boats and taught him. And his girlfriend helped him." The half smile told him she relished the reminiscence.

"Did he get in trouble?"

"Not the way you mean. No cops." She could've lashed out at him for that question, but her expression turned wistful. "Jordan's basically a good kid. He's not slow, but he sees things concretely, and he acts on impulse. He trusts the wrong people."

She was being too hopeful by far, but he'd see where this led. "So he might have gone along with what Sudsy Pettit told him about the deliveries."

"I think that's it. And when he learned what was really going on, he panicked."

Silverware clattered with the clearing of the vacated booth, and Juliana started.

When the busboy had hustled the dirty dishes off to the kitchen, Rick said, "Your brother's only part of why I wanted to see you today." He set down his empty glass.

"I don't have much time."

"You skipped classes this morning. More investigating this afternoon?"

Her mouth tightened. She slapped her napkin on her lap. "What is it you want?"

Their orders arrived. A veggie roll-up for Juliana and a turkey sub for him. Averting her eyes, Juliana bit into her sandwich with an eagerness that betrayed her hunger.

Cheered by her capitulation, Rick lifted his sub. He stopped dead at the sight of her tongue dabbing at salad dressing on her upper lip. Focus, he told himself. Distance. "Let's suppose Jordan has hidden somewhere. I assume you know the possibilities. Since you can't find him, no one can."

"Maybe. So tell me about this El Águila." Her eyes narrowed with skepticism.

"El Águila is a Mexican cartel and also the soubriquet of its head. The Eagle is a ruthless man, no way noble like the bird of prey he's named for." He wouldn't tell her the U. S. had nada on his real name or description.

"A Mexican drug lord? In Maine? Please." Although she scoffed, furrows appeared between her eyes.

"The border between Mexico and the U.S. is

more secure, and the wars among the drug cartels and with the Mexican army are more vicious. El Águila still operates in his native land but he has long arms that have reached into the Northeast, including the coast of Maine."

Her eyes widened with comprehension. "With its long, porous coastline."

"Exactly. Lots of small harbors and coves and vacation homes with deep-water docks. The distance cuts into his bottom line, but don't cry over this cutthroat's expenses. They smuggle heroin and cocaine into the country. On the return trip, they take guns and explosives to continue the violence in Mexico."

"A vicious cycle." Her gaze flickered with concern. Probably wondering where her baby brother fit into the gang.

"Don't underestimate the danger. If Carlos Olívas, his lieutenant here in the Northeast, thinks you know or have evidence of their drug and gun smuggling, or if he thinks you know where your brother is, he'll . . . *pressure* you."

"You seem to know him well." Her lips curved, but in a teeth-baring challenge. Not what Rick had in mind when he wished for her smile.

"You got me there. Olívas and I have never met, but I do know him." And what he could do to Jordan.

"What could he think I know?" Her voice was reedy, her eyes wide.

"It looked like they were searching for something in Jordan's place. Perhaps he has evidence against them."

"That's what you're hoping. And you think this

Olívas might suspect Jordan gave it to me." With her fork, she poked shredded lettuce back into her wrap sandwich. "I don't suppose the DEA would go so far as to keep *pressuring* me to make it look that way to Carlos, would they? Would *you*?"

Rick blinked at her cynical deduction. Hell, she still thought the worst of him. "I would never put a civilian in that kind of danger."

"Perhaps." She put down her half-finished sandwich and sipped her sparkling water.

"I'll help you find your brother. I can't promise not to arrest him, but I do promise to keep him safe. And you can help me uncover whatever it is he knows or has hidden."

After wiping her mouth with her napkin, she laid it beside her plate. "Agent Cruz—"

"Rick. My first name is Rick." He offered her his best smile, the one that charmed females from nine to ninety.

"I don't have any idea where Jordan is. I know nothing about evidence and I doubt this Olívas believes I do."

"Be careful. You wouldn't like his kind of pressure. Olívas enjoys hurting people."

"I believe you, but I can't trust strangers with my brother's life." She dug a dollar bill from her bag and shoved it under her plate. She slid from the booth.

Rick remained seated as she strode to the cashier. A sudden craving for a smoke had him popping a mint.

He was a man who loved women, and they usually loved him. From childhood, he knew that his looks and smile gave him an edge with females.

In return, they charmed him. He liked their company, their scents, their soft skin, their musical voices, the intricacies of their minds. Age didn't matter. The mutual admiration ranged from his ancient Basque grandmother to the smallest tot. Even at times, his sisters.

But not Juliana Paris. Exactly like the guys had said. Shit.

After she swung through the luncheonette's glass door, Rick paid his check and followed her at a distance. He'd keep an eye on her as far as her car. It would be tragic if stubbornness placed her in harm's way. But her refusal seemed like more than stubbornness, more like distrust. Did Juliana distrust the DEA or cops in general? And why?

A steady stream of people strolled Congress Street. Students and older tweedy professorial types. Street people in ragged layers and office workers in business layers. No one strode more purposefully than Juliana.

She turned right at the side street and waited to cross. He wove among the few passing cars and pedestrians lined up at an ATM to duck in Computer Fix's doorway. Around the display window, he observed her progress. Keeping an eye on her dark red backpack, he treated himself to the sight of her trim hips swaying with her brisk stride.

A green van with smoked glass windows screeched to a stop before Juliana. Two men jumped out. Blind to the street drama, the foot traffic parted around the van and proceeded on their way. Horns blared and irate motorists shouted.

One man grabbed Juliana by the right arm. The other gesticulated and spoke rapidly to her. Traffic noises and distance prevented him from hearing what the man said.

Adrenaline surged. Rick didn't wait to see what would happen next.

Pistol in hand, he raced down the street.

- 4 -

Juliana's heart pounded and her throat tightened. She twisted, trying to wrench from the man's grasp. If only she could swing her bag. "Let me go!"

He was barely taller than she and hefty, but more lumpish than muscular. With a sharp pinch like oversized pliers, his hand clamped tightly on her elbow. The other man was taller and stoop-shouldered, with sunken eyes and a drooping moustache. Abruptly he glanced behind her. He scowled and beckoned to his companion.

One minute Juliana was struggling to get free, and the next her kidnappers leaped into their van and sped away.

Two strong, hard hands gripped her shoulders and turned her. "Are you all right? Those bastards didn't hurt you?" Ricardo Cruz stared at her as if he could see inside for the answer to his question.

"I'm fine." She stepped back. She panted with rasping breaths and her knees shook. "They . . . just wanted to talk to me."

Adjusting his jacket over his holstered pistol, Cruz shot a skeptical glance heavenward. He pulled out his notepad and jotted something.

The van's license number maybe, but she wouldn't give him the satisfaction of asking. His running to her rescue and his strong hands on her shoulders made her feel safe, no longer imperiled. Frowning, she glanced away. She wouldn't rely on this man or like him.

A few passing students smiled their way, apparently taking them for quarrelling lovers. A car horn beeped once and then blared the driver's irritation at the delay. Ack, they still stood in the street and the light had changed again. Extricating herself from Cruz, she hurried on. After all, she did have places to go. And she didn't want him to see how frightened she was. She couldn't stop trembling, and her stomach still churned like a blender.

"Next you're going to tell me those guys only wanted directions to Freeport." His long strides easily kept pace with hers. "That they weren't interested in your brother."

Shaking her head, she slanted him a glance. "Did you know them?"

"One. I've seen him before with Olívas. I couldn't see the face of the one who held you. Could you describe him? Or identify his picture?"

Juliana huffed and shook her head as she picked up speed. "He was behind me."

Though the men's cinnamon skin, shades darker than Cruz's burnished hue, could have belonged to any of several ethnic groups, Droopy Mustache's accent marked him as Hispanic. She suppressed a shudder at the memory of his menacing tones.

Both fell silent while they dodged among a throng of pedestrians. A young man wearing a shirt that proclaimed, "Save Our Finny Friends," jostled her.

Cruz grasped her arm and scowled at the kid.

She'd pull away but it'd cause another scene. His hand was firm but gentle on her arm, warm and reassuring, dammit. She inhaled his warm, masculine scent, fringed with mint. Beyond that sensual charm, his protectiveness and apparent concern for her—and her foolish brother—tempted her to like him, to trust him.

She *wanted* to trust him. But she shouldn't. Couldn't.

Once beside her car, they stopped, but he maintained his firm grip on her arm. "Are you going to tell me what the Mexicans wanted?"

She raised her chin. "They asked me about Jordan. I told them I don't know where he is, and he didn't give me anything. That's the end of it." If she repeated it enough, maybe she'd believe her own story.

"You're more naïve than my baby sister if you believe that. Those guys have been following you." He held up his other hand to stay her protest. His voice rose with frustration. "I saw the lie in your eyes earlier when you denied it. These are dangerous men. You must believe me. They want information and they'll hurt you to get it."

"I know nothing and have nothing they could want." She freed her arm and unlocked her car. "Now, if you'll excuse me, I have *investigating* to do." She tossed in her backpack and slid inside. Dammit, she fumbled the key in the ignition. Finally the poor, overworked engine caught and she pulled away from the curb.

Those men, at least someone in their van, had followed her before on the way to the bank. This time they approached her in public view.

What would they do next?

The memory of that vice-like grip was her answer. A shudder swept through her.

Finally she had a lead. *Finny.* The name on the T-shirt had clicked in her memory. Finny was Jordan's friend on the Vinson dragger. She ignored her nerves jumping like accounting numbers on a page at midnight as she drove to Portland the next day.

The DEA had released Jordan's apartment, and the manager wanted her brother out. After packing Jordan's sparse belongings, she aimed her aged Sentra for the docks. She'd never gone to the headquarters before, but had filled in at Vinson's Portsmouth office. In front of her the Portland Fish Pier buildings sprawled over several piers.

A turn onto Commercial Street put the docks on her right, with ferries and commercial shipping jockeying for space amid restaurants and sailmakers. Beyond the hubbub, a north wind fluttered white petticoats on the verdigris surface of Casco Bay. On her left, locals and tourists ducked in the quaint shops, brew pubs, and galleries of the Old Port.

She spotted her destination on the last wharf past the Casco Bay Lines ferry terminal. Vinson Seafood, Shipping & Marina. Fishing craft with derricks and netting bobbed on the waves beside the marina. On the pavement by the boat storage building, two yachts bigger than three-story houses awaited the season on tripod stands.

She eased into a parking slot near the old brick building. The engine gave a little cough as it chugged to a halt. The car had given her good service, considering Molly had purchased it second hand, but soon she'd have to invest in new transportation.

If only she knew where her mother was so she could share her concerns. Delete that. What a waste of time. Molly would refuse to worry and insist Jordan was fine.

She checked the rearview and side mirrors. Twice during her drive, a red sports car had appeared in her rearview mirror. No sign of it now. But neither the drug gang nor the DEA would use such an obvious vehicle.

Scooping up her purse, she slid out and locked up. The calendar might say it was spring, but warm weather wouldn't hit the Maine coast anytime soon. She zipped her parka and smoothed her skirt before striding to the building entrance.

Inside, a cavernous office stretched the length of the building. In front was a reception counter and behind it a maze of workspaces manned by people at computers.

A young woman in a Vinson logo polo shirt greeted her at the reception desk. In a few moments she directed Juliana toward the rear of the building and the office of Wesley Vinson.

Carpeted in a deep forest green pile, the office was dominated by a venerable oak desk. A tenor voice came from the leather chair facing a window.

"No, they haven't come in. Maybe sometime around noon."

Not wanting to eavesdrop but uncertain about how to make her presence known, she hovered around the door.

"Piece of cake," the disembodied voice said. "I'll call you."

"Hello, they sent me back here," she called when she heard a click.

"Ahoy there." The chair swiveled to face her, revealing a ruddy-cheeked, husky man. Fitting the receiver on the telephone console, he rose and flashed a smile as wide and white as a seagull's wing. "Sorry I didn't hear you come in."

She went forward and introduced herself.

He took her hand in both of his big, smooth ones. "The gods of my Viking ancestors have sent you to my rescue, Juliana Paris. My solitary confinement authorizing bill payments was approaching mind-numbing status. Rather be out on my boat."

"I'm happy to save you, but I hope you'll return the favor." He seemed personable, this fortyish blond, a casual Maine executive in creased khakis and L.L. Bean boat shoes.

He ushered her to a club chair. Choosing an adjacent one rather than his executive throne, he propped one leg on the other knee. "What can I do for you?"

She drew a calming breath. "My brother works for you sometimes, on the *Following Sea*." She explained what had happened with her brother and the DEA.

"DEA agents came here to see me about Jordan.

I don't recall him personally, but my captain vouched for him. So you don't think he's mixed up with these drug gangsters?"

"No, I don't." She shook her head emphatically. "But more than that, I'm worried about him. I think he's hiding from them, and I want to find him first."

"Isn't that dangerous?" He bent forward. "The gang and all."

Why did everyone have to remind her of the obvious? "He's my brother."

"Then how can I help you?"

Here goes nothing. "Jordan has a friend on board the *Following Sea*, a guy named Finny. I thought Jordan might be staying with him."

"Finny, huh?" Vinson smoothed his dark gold hair. "Name doesn't ring any bells. I'll check the employee files. With a fishing fleet and the marina, we have dozens of employees. Since my old man turned the reins over, I've been trying to build the company."

The marina had new-looking buildings. "Nice marina. That must do a good business."

"Diversifying is my plan. Not much profit in North Atlantic fishing these days."

When he moved to the computer and started punching keys, she all but wept with gratitude. Here was the first person to help her, to grant her the credibility to do this her way. "I really appreciate this, Mr. Vinson."

"It's Wes." His grin banished the rest of her nerves.

"Wes," she repeated with a smile. "You'll find me in that list too. Temps-R-Us has sent me to your Portsmouth office a few times."

He winked. "It's my loss I never dropped in when you were there. Maybe I'll have them send you here next time."

"I wouldn't mind." Wes's light-hearted flirting didn't annoy her the way Cruz's magnetic sensuality did.

Vinson trailed a finger down the screen. "No Finny in the list. Nothing that even resembles it."

"Can you sort them differently? Maybe it's a first name?"

A few more screen flickers yielded a name and address. "Maybe this one. Finnegan Farnham. In Saco. Guess it wouldn't hurt to give you the address." He jotted it down.

Her pulse did a jig. "This is my first real lead."

"Whoa, it may be a bum lead. Farnham's not in port." By his eyes, crinkles fanned out in commiseration. "He shipped out a few days ago on the *Sea Worthy*. Won't return until the first or second week in April. I'd try to radio, but Old Sparky's too low-tech. The boat's probably too far out for me to rouse her from here."

"Thank you. You helped. More than you know."

Vinson walked her outside into the cool spring sunshine and pointed out an approaching green fishing boat, derricks and nets making it look top-heavy. "That's the seiner I'm waiting for, the *Sea Jaunty*. Coming in with a good load of herring. It's a smaller boat than the one your brother usually crews on, only about eighty feet." He scratched his head. "If you can stick around town awhile, I'll take you to lunch."

Lunch in the Old Port with Wes Vinson would be more elegant than hers downtown with Rick

Cruz. If she hadn't already eaten, she'd enjoy a meal with him. He didn't get under her skin like a certain other man. "I'd love to, but I have to get back to Portsmouth."

Before she rolled out of the parking lot, Vinson waved her to a halt. "I just had a thought. The *Sea Worthy* will sail into Rockland and Belfast off and on to sell their catch. If you still want to talk to Farnham, I could leave a message for him to call you." His lips curved. "Then maybe I could call you too."

"I'd appreciate that." After reciting her cell number and promising to go out with him, she drove away. In the meantime, she could check out Finny's place.

Wes Vinson watched Juliana's small car disappear down Commercial before he went inside. Back in his office, he closed the door and pulled out his cell phone.

When the call was answered, he said, "What did you find?"

"Nothing helpful. My men tell me the Paris *chica* just left your office. She is looking for her *idiota* of a brother?"

"She doesn't know where he is but she knows something. We don't have much time. The Feds are moving in. They searched the kid's apartment."

"Perhaps she needs a scare."

The smile in the other man's voice chilled Wes Vinson. "What are you planning?"

But he was talking to dead air.

SUSAN VAUGHAN

An hour later, Juliana slumped in her car seat. The neighbors in Finny's apartment building had seen no one in his apartment since Saturday—the sailing date of the *Sea Worthy*. It'd been worth a try. On a sigh, she headed south on the interstate. She still had the old girlfriend to find. For a distraction, she turned up the radio and sang along with Adele.

Until she spotted the red sports car behind her.

Rick steered back into the slow lane. Damn, why hadn't he used a government sedan instead of driving his Corvette? Juliana spotted him this time, and she might have earlier. Both charm and stealth failed him. Hell of an Invisible Man.

And he wanted a cigarette. Bad. He popped a mint into his mouth.

As a SEAL, he'd learned self-control and patience in the worst circumstances. Waiting to perform a rescue operation once, he lay on his belly for six hours in a steaming, bug-infested swamp. He remained dead still while lizards and poisonous snakes and the devil knew what else slithered across his back and legs and the enemy marched past within inches. As a DEA agent, he'd sat for hours across the table from a drug dealer until the guy cracked from the mere pressure of the interminable silence.

But this female could make him jumpy with a flash of her green eyes or a snide remark in her throaty voice. What was it about her? Not just her curvy figure and snapping eyes, but something underneath. That sense of loyalty and support he wished he had from his family.

Guanajo. What a turkey he was. For now, he would simply follow her to protect her. Sooner or later she'd uncover a lead or decide to work with him. He had to be patient.

Patient, hell. He spat out a juicy Spanish epithet.

Keeping her old blue Sentra in sight, he looked around for suspicious vehicles. Nada. Now that Olívas's men knew he'd made them, they would use a different vehicle, not the van. He'd sweet-talked Laurel in Intelligence into rushing the trace on the van's license number. Stolen vehicle. No lead there.

At the York exit, more traffic poured onto the multi-lane interstate. All the extra vehicles, like fish in a school, helped to conceal him. He and Juliana breezed through the tollbooth with their electronic passes. When they neared Kittery, he pulled closer to her.

When she accelerated speed, he hung back so as not to crowd her. The moment he did, a black Lincoln swerved around him and pulled up beside her. Shit. Olívas's men. Maybe Olívas too, the sadistic slime. He accelerated past an SUV. He had to catch up. If the bastards spotted him on their tail, maybe they'd ease off Juliana.

A solid chain of cars cruised by him in the passing lane and blocked his move.

Stuck behind a Volvo wagon, Rick slammed his hand on the steering wheel. It was like going backwards in slow motion. What were those bastards up to?

At last, his chance came and he yanked the wheel left to pull around the Volvo and make it three cars closer. Juliana glanced to her left. She immediately accelerated. Must have realized her plight.

Rick gunned it but a Chevy Silverado swerved in front of him. The pickup's height and size blocked his view. He had no police radio or siren and no means of clearing the way. He stewed, as helpless as though bound and gagged. "What the hell!"

The pickup shot back into the right lane in time for him to see the Lincoln swerve in behind Juliana. In tandem, like racers on a one-lane course, Juliana's Sentra and the Lincoln zoomed across the Piscataqua River Bridge from Maine into New Hampshire.

With Rick trapped two cars behind in the left lane.

The Sentra made an unexpected right and zipped out the downtown Portsmouth exit. Swaying on its shocks, the Lincoln made the turn, a couple of car lengths behind her.

Where was Juliana going? She hugged the exit curve like an Indy racer. Her Sentra had less power but more agility than the Lincoln. How the hell did she learn to drive that way?

Boxed in, Rick couldn't make the exit. His last sight of both cars chilled him to the marrow.

Out of the Lincoln's open window jutted a long black gun muzzle.

- 5 -

Pops and thunks slamming into the car's rear jolted Juliana against the shoulder harness. Hands clammy, she gripped the steering wheel. Her ears hummed and her heart raced faster than the Sentra's motor.

Oh, my God, they were shooting at her!

More bullets rammed into the rear end. Plastic shattered. A bumper or a taillight.

Her stomach roiled. Her throat tightened, threatening to choke off air from her dry mouth. No, no, she had to pull it together. She could do this.

Think!

It was like on the racetrack. At least one of Molly's men had been worthwhile. But her main advantage was that she knew the tangled, one-way streets of Portsmouth, and her pursuers didn't. She hoped.

She yanked the steering wheel to make the hard right onto Deer. Then an immediate sharp left to High.

The black sedan dropped back. Still in pursuit but less aggressive.

Traffic in downtown Portsmouth bustled with tourists and local shoppers. More pedestrians than cars. A tour group crossed the street behind her. They blocked the sedan.

More random twists and turns, and she swung into a parking garage and out the other side. Then a left to Hanover and Maplewood.

She checked the mirror. No sign of the long black car. She rotated her shoulders and flexed her aching fingers. Trembling shook her all over but she could drive. The drug gang might know where she lived, but maybe she could make it before they caught her.

How stupid to have kept her eye on the red sports car. Just when she'd celebrated losing him, the black car appeared like a storm cloud overtaking her. Jordan's mess was a hell of a lot more dangerous that she'd realized. Maybe Cruz was right.

Within minutes she reached her building's parking lot. She raced up to the second floor and safety. She bobbled the key and nearly dropped it. Finally she made it inside and slammed home the dead bolt. Resting her head against the cool wood of the door, she listened to the drumming of her heart and choked back tears.

A fist pounded on the door.

Pulse in the stratosphere, she jumped aside. "I called the police. They're on their way."

"Good, saves me from calling them. Let me in, Juliana."

Her heart slowed to mach one. She leaned

against the wall and drew a deep, cleansing breath. Now she knew who owned the red sports car.

She flicked back the lock and opened the door. To conceal her relief at seeing him, she scowled. "Agent Cruz, what the hell did you think you were doing?"

"What *I* was doing?" He stepped inside and kicked the door shut. His dark brows bunched, and his black eyes blazed with fury. "Only sticking close to protect you. But you lost me and gave those guys their opening."

She waved her arms. "Protect me? *Protect me?* You led them to me. They probably shot at me because of you! I . . ."

A Nor'easter of emotion hit her. She shook like a sapling in the storm, and tears fell like rain.

Without comment, Cruz pulled her to him. He wrapped his arms around her and held her to his warm, hard chest. He rubbed circles on her back.

"I'm s-s-sorry," she blubbered. "I never c-c-cry. I don't know what's come over me." When she tried to step back, he pressed her closer. A white handkerchief magically floated before her eyes. She wouldn't think about how protected she felt and how good his arms felt or how she liked his minty scent.

"Happens when you're not used to being shot at."

"Oh." After blowing her nose into the soft cotton, she looked up.

Rick Cruz wasn't the handsomest man she'd ever met. Right. Okay, maybe he was. At the moment he wasn't smiling. He gazed at her with candid concern. There again was that protective attitude.

But he was just doing his job. She shouldn't read anything into it.

"I'm all right now." She edged from his embrace. "I'm sorry I yelled at you."

"You were scared." He leaned against the door. "How did you learn to drive like that?"

She lifted one shoulder in dismissal. "A man I used to know worked at a race track. He showed me a few maneuvers." She started to turn from the door toward the living room, but Cruz took her hands and held her in place.

"I don't hear sirens," he said. "Did you really phone the cops?"

"No, I just said that to scare off the jerks in that black car."

"Then you ought to phone them now."

"You're right. Those men shot at me. There are bullets in my car." The statement churned her stomach.

"Looks like they hit the gas tank. There's gas running onto the parking lot. You're lucky it didn't blow."

She tugged but he held her fast. "How can I phone if you're holding my hands?"

"Have you looked at your apartment?"

He released her and she pivoted. The upheaval in Jordan's flat couldn't begin to match what a tornado had wrought on hers. Her vision distorted like a funhouse mirror. "Oh, God!"

Cruz guided her to a chair and gently pushed her into it. He picked up the phone from the floor and punched in 911.

"Now, Juliana, will you let me help you?"

"Whoo-ee, Macmillan's not gonna like this." Donovan drawled out a western-flavored expletive. Rick had phoned to inform his office of the latest developments. "He's been kickin' ass about the lack of progress on Operation Fish Truck."

"Yeah, well, tell him the facts and get back to me." Rick hit disconnect on his cell.

Juliana was still talking to one of the Portsmouth cops, but she kept casting glances at the disaster in her home. Probably anxious to put things away. She didn't seem capable of absolute stillness. She twisted fingers together or tapped a foot or straightened something. The nervous energy humming around her fascinated him.

"I don't know what else is missing, officer," she said. "They might have taken my cat. I don't see him anywhere."

Possible, but the most likely outcome would be to find the creature's mutilated corpse tucked away somewhere. Or maybe the cat was hiding. Shouldn't be hard to search an apartment the size of a saltine cracker. Rick started in the bedroom. Even with furniture upside down and drawers and closets inside out, it was apparent she lived simply. Basic furnishings, plants, and books. A few butterfly knickknacks. Tiny TV, not the latest computer, older flip phone. Tight budget, this woman.

A new voice brought him from the bedroom. At the door stood a flashy female holding a cat the size of his year-old nephew. She handed the placid animal to Juliana. "Here's Speedy, hon."

Speedy? This brute? Rick rubbed a hand across his mouth to cover a smile.

"Oh, you're safe, Speedy, you're safe," Juliana crooned into the cat's fur.

The soothing tone and her doting expression darted prickles on his skin and sent heat south. He clenched his jaw.

"I found him sitting in the hall," the woman said.

"Yes, ma'am." The Portsmouth detective bobbed his head like a puppet on a string. Apparently he was stuck for more questions. All three cops could barely keep their tongues from hanging out at Juliana's friend's voluptuous presence in a black leotard wrapped with a slinky leopard-print skirt.

"This is my neighbor, Venice Aaron," Juliana told them. "Thanks, Venice."

"No problem, hon." Venice's eyes widened. "What hurricane hit this place?"

"Burglars. Speedy must have sneaked out when they broke in." She deposited the cat on the floor.

With a disdainful meow, the animal strolled with regal grace to the bedroom.

"Burglars, huh?" Her dusky skin paled a shade, and her gaze darted around the room. "I knocked, but you weren't home. Then I had a hair appointment."

"Hey, Ms. Aaron," Rick said, joining the group, "that hairdresser is worth whatever you paid. Very foxy."

Venice preened and smiled seductively. "You're looking mighty fine yourself. I'm Venice to my friends."

Juliana swallowed the spurt of irritation. For all she cared, that man could follow Venice home. Never mind that in his jeans and khaki safari shirt he looked good enough to eat. Before she could return the conversation to the situation at hand, Cruz did it for her.

"Venice, what time did you find the cat?"

"Two hours ago. Everything looked normal." She propped fists on hips. "You think those burglars were in here when I knocked?"

"Possible."

The Portsmouth detective scrawled in his notebook.

"How did they get in?" Juliana asked. "The windows are okay, and the door wasn't damaged."

Cruz nodded as if in approval she'd noticed the lack of damage. "They picked the lock with professional tools that left only faint scratches. They knew you weren't home."

"And I guess I know how. The black Lincoln."

One swift stride brought him to her side. He slid an arm around her shoulders.

She began to pull free, but the commanding spark in his eyes held her in place. Against her will, she absorbed comfort from his embrace.

"We lifted some prints," the detective said, "but I don't have much hope about that. We have all we need for now, ma'am. We'll do everything we can to catch these burglars. Between us and the D—"

"We'll contact you about the car," Cruz said.

The detective tipped his head in agreement.

How could she have forgotten about the car? She couldn't get to work and to class without it. She couldn't search for Jordan. "My car, when will I get it back?"

"I'll call you when we're done with it. But that heap's gonna need work before you can drive it again."

She groaned, visualizing the dollar signs in the mechanic's eyes. New gas tank. New taillights. Body work. Even with what insurance would cover, she couldn't afford repairs *and* school. Her credit card was maxed out.

The detective turned to Venice. "Ma'am, we'd appreciate it if we could take your fingerprints so we can eliminate them from those we lifted in here."

"You bet, Detective, sugar. You come with me." On her way out, she said to Juliana, "I'll come back and help you straighten up."

"Not necessary," Cruz replied smoothly before Juliana could. "She's in good hands."

"I can see that, doll." Venice's Cheshire-cat grin told Juliana that her friend missed none of what just transpired. Including the agent's possessive arm around her.

Now that the others had left, she scooted away from him until she came up against the kitchen divider. "What was *that* all about?"

Dark eyes wide in feigned innocence, he ambled closer. "It seemed best if Venice thought I was your guy rather than DEA."

"She already knows about my brother and the DEA." His thoughtful gesture surprised her. Maybe she shouldn't have spoken so sharply. He *was* trying to help. She stepped away, but he held her with that compelling dark gaze.

He wasn't touching her, but she was locked in place as if he'd caged her against the counter. She shouldn't be attracted to this man, with his effortless charm. He'd take and take and never give, just like Molly's men.

But he met her eyes, as if willing her to trust. Maybe she could trust *him*, for the support and protection every cell in her body yearned for. A little. But no way would she trust the DEA with her brother's life.

She turned away and knelt by the bookcase, gathering a few volumes from the carpet. Two she set on the top shelf, a third belonged on the next one down.

"If people think we're together as lovers, it'll be easier to protect you." He lifted three books and handed them to her. "My boss thought it best if I protect you undercover. To draw out the bad guys."

"It doesn't make sense. Olívas must know the DEA is looking for Jordan." He probably wasn't leveling with her, but what did she expect? She set the books on the shelves.

"Perhaps. But the only way to find out the reason is to locate your brother or uncover what he knows." He handed her three more books. "Alphabetical by author. You probably keep all your kitchen spices in the same order."

Taking the books from him, she nodded. "Venice tells me it's obsessive, but how else would I find what I need?"

He laughed and handed her the last. "My way's looser. A pile here, a pile there. But I know what's in every one."

The day's turmoil still churned in her system. "What do you think they were looking for? And why did they try to kill me?"

He slid a glass butterfly from her hand and placed it on the high shelf she was eyeing. "Those sleazeballs don't miss. They were aiming low to frighten you."

Only when he took her hands in his big ones did she realize hers were trembling.

"It worked. I'm scared to death." And angry and violated and soiled, as if the searchers had defiled her personally. Without Rick's strong, comforting presence she'd be a basket case.

"As for what they were after, either something they think Jordan might have given you or left in his apartment."

"What? A name? A list of their crimes?"

"We don't have enough to go on yet to hazard a guess. I need you to tell me everything you've found out on your own. We'll go from there." He chafed her hands in his, warming more than her fingers. "Let's finish here, and you'll feel better."

An hour later, they'd returned the living room and kitchen to a semblance of order. Juliana put the broken items—mostly plant pots, glassware, and a few ceramic butterflies—in a trash bag. She didn't care about most of it except for the butterflies, mementoes from Molly's travels, reminders to keep herself grounded.

"Why dump plants and potting soil all over the place? What would I hide there?"

"Anything from a microfilm to a microchip to a microtape. Who knows?"

When they reached the bedroom, they found the cat sound asleep on a pile of sweaters.

"Speedy, huh?" he said.

"For Speedy Gonzalez, the mouse in the cartoons." She scooped up the quilt and sheets from the floor and piled them on the mattress.

"So you do have a thing against Latinos. Slow

and lazy, like this cat, is that what you think?" He dropped a crumpled lampshade and a cracked bulb in the trash bag.

Dammit she'd have to launder everything. Then her brain registered his words. Her mouth rounded and her cheeks burned at the inference he'd drawn. "Oh no, I didn't mean— It's only— He was such a wild speed demon as a kitten that I—"

A glance at him silenced her fumbled apology. "You're kidding, aren't you?"

"Lighten up, Juliana." With a wicked smile, he ran a finger along her chin. Tiny bonfires sprang up in his wake.

She jerked away and lifted a broken ceramic pot. "Well, pardon me if I can't joke when everything's gone to hell."

"We'll find Jordan. The gang wouldn't be so worried if he was dead. And they may have yanked all your belongings from the drawers and closets, but only a few items got broken. They slit upholstery but not these luscious confections at my feet."

Her gaze swept the scattered lingerie and other clothing. Her cheeks practically broiled. "I can do the rest of this by myself. Thanks for your help."

"You don't want me folding your bras and panties? A teddy, too. Very sexy."

She backed away. "Look, we have to work together, I agree, to find my brother. And in a crazy way it makes sense for us to pretend to be—" She stopped, unable to utter the word.

"Lovers."

"—*close*. But why can't you be my cousin or something instead?"

"Hard to picture a cousin being that devoted." He shook his head. It's only pretend."

"And pretending is all it's going to be. I need to know my brother's all right. I have my own goals. That means not getting involved with . . . anyone." Especially a handsome man who could charm the colors off a butterfly's wings. And throw her brother into jail where God knew what could happen to him.

"I understand *no*, and I promise you'll be safe." He scooped up more lingerie. With a graceful Zorro bow, he dumped the undies in her arms.

"You'd better go. I have to call around and see what I can do about transportation for the next week or so."

"No problem. Chauffeur and bodyguard Ricardo Cruz at your service." He snagged his jacket and ambled to the door.

"What do you mean?" She shoved her discount outlet underwear in a top drawer before following him. She'd launder and organize everything later. The chore would keep her busy, body and mind.

"Protecting you. What's next on the agenda for finding your brother?"

"No, you don't have to do that." How strong would her resistance be if she rode in that small sports car with Rick every day? And when did he become *Rick*? "There must be some other way, Agent Cruz. I can manage."

"I can protect you, and we can work together. Or are we competing? It can't be both."

She sighed. He was right. "It's just I'm not used to anyone helping me."

"Your friend will be happy. She'll think we're a

couple. Can you play your part convincingly?" He hooked a finger beneath her chin and brushed his thumb over her lower lip.

- 6 -

Later that afternoon, Rick contacted Holt Donovan.

"At first the GS went ballistic," Donovan told him, "but Jake and I convinced Macmillan to allow you to escort the Paris woman. That puts her in protective custody."

Better them than Rick facing the Group Supervisor on that issue. He blew out a breath. "I owe you one, Holt. Juliana does need protection. What else?"

"Nothing yet on the bullets. Portland PD found the Lincoln in an alley. Reported stolen the day before the ambush. No prints. Maybe the lab techs will find something."

"Jake have any leads on the smuggled weapons?"

"He and one of the other ATF guys are out trying to track how Olivas and company ship the weapons north and where they store them until they have a boat. Word is this shipment contains Bushmaster semi-automatic handguns as well as assault rifles, AK-47s and AR-15s. 7.62 and .223 caliber bullets. And a block of C-4. Jake can tell you more later."

Rick emitted a low whistle. "Powerful weapons and nasty explosives."

As he disconnected, he dragged in a lungful of air and got back to work.

He had semi-success tracking down Jordan's former girlfriend. The girl's parents gave him her phone number at UCLA, but she hadn't seen Jordan since graduation.

Then there was Juliana. She refused a safe house, insisting she needed to remain where her brother could find her. And she insisted on following her regular jogging routine. After he reminded her she couldn't outrun a bullet, she agreed to accept him as a running partner.

One of the local agents was letting him stay in a furnished apartment over his garage for the duration. A shorter commute than from Boston made up for not having his stuff. But the main perk was seeing Juliana early in the morning, cheeks glowing pink in her heart-shaped face and her bright hair caressing her shoulders. Torture too. He was here to find the brother, to arrest Olívas, not to hook up with a woman connected to crooks. He shouldn't want her. But all he wanted to do was carry her off to bed. A couch. The floor.

Worse, Wes Vinson had requested Juliana to sub for his secretary for the rest of the week. She allowed a light kiss between them every day when he dropped her off—part of their cover. Right. He tried and failed to put her sweet taste out of his mind.

He couldn't object to her working at Vinson Seafood. Couldn't tell her Vinson was one of the prime suspects in Operation Fish Truck. But every day, fear for her twisted inside him—fear she'd be handed over to Olívas as leverage to flush out her brother.

So far all El Águila's men were doing was tailing her. This time they were legal. A rented tan Ford. A DEA tail kept track of them and reported to Rick.

Frigid rain and cloudy skies had plagued them the past two days, but on Friday morning, only a few wintry clouds splotched the pale blue sky. Rick squinted at the glare through the windshield. Persuading Juliana to go had taken the rest of the week, but finally the two of them headed Down East. She'd pled a previously scheduled commitment, and Vinson didn't object.

The weather wasn't all that had defrosted. Sharing the morning jogs and the daily commute seemed to make her more at ease with him. Less suspicious of his motives. Nah, probably not. But she softened enough to carry on normal conversations. He'd take it.

He glanced at her. She sat beside him, visibly humming with anticipation and hope. Something— her intensity, her dry wit, her compact curves—tied him in knots. Thinking about her made him hard as his nine-millimeter.

She pointed at the hood. "What's with the horns? Whose truck is this?"

"My borrowed undercover vehicle. Belongs to another agent. Cowboy from the Wild, Wild West."

These wheels weren't as inconspicuous as he'd like. The gunmetal Silverado suited Maine, but the cow horns on the hood stuck out like a palm tree in Alaska.

She smoothed her left hand across the wide console between them. "I like it. Not as racy as the sports car, but more room."

He enfolded her cold hand. "You should check out the license plate. *HI YO.*"

"*Silver, away*?" With a laugh, she tugged free her hand and opened her bag. She pulled her hair up and wrapped it with a stretchy band. The springy curls invited touching.

Rick flexed his fingers on the steering wheel. "Still no response from your calls to your uncle and your mother?"

"Uncle Grady hasn't returned my calls. I left a personal message for Molly on my machine, but I don't know if she's called to hear it. No message back."

"It blows me away that you call your mother Molly."

"When I turned thirteen, she insisted. She said it made her feel younger."

Knowing more about her mother would give him insight into the daughter. "You've hinted at her traveling and being irresponsible."

She raised a hand against the sun's glare. "Ever since my dad's death, she's lived only for the day or for some charming man's pie-in-the-sky plan. My dad was one of those dreamers. He lost all his money—*our* money—several times. He had big ideas and worked hard, but things never went his way."

"Is accounting a way to prevent that disaster for others? Or for yourself?"

"Something like that, I suppose. It's what I'm good at."

"And your mom?"

"She finds these happy-go-lucky, handsome charmers who fill her head with promises of a rosy future. Sometimes they lavish her with trips and expensive gifts, but most of the time she ends up alone and penniless. Until the next man comes along." She frowned as if uncertain she should've opened up so much.

Maybe he had only the false intimacy of the pickup's cab to thank, but whatever. "Doesn't sound like her independent daughter."

"I hope not. Don't get me wrong. I love Molly, but we are very different."

"My *mamá* would roast me with the *arroz con pollo* if I ever called her Ashley."

She laughed. "Ashley. That doesn't sound very Cuban."

"She's as Anglo as you. My parents met in Miami when she was singing in nightclubs and my *papá* was waiting tables and going to medical school."

"So your dad is a doctor?"

"A surgeon. The best in Miami." Rudy used to say he wanted to be a physician too. Until he chose a wrong path. Before Rick could get too maudlin, she spoke again.

"Do you have any more information on Jordan?"

The kid was probably involved up to his hairline, but he wouldn't tell her his suspicions. He couldn't squash her faith in her brother. He could use family loyalty like hers. "The sense is that he's a little fish and worth netting only for what he knows."

"The same reason the drug gang wants him, I suppose." She cast him a fretful glance.

"Try not to worry too much about Jordan. If they had him, they wouldn't be following you. Think positive."

"Easy for you to say." She twisted in the seat to face him. "Tell me something, Agent Cruz, with all the slime you see in your business, how do you maintain such an upbeat attitude? Or is it a cover for your real feelings?"

Her perception surprised him. Not something he'd put into words. "If I didn't know better, I'd think you could see inside me."

"So you do have a dark side?"

"Not really. At least, not for long. Sometimes looking on the bright side slides me past the dark patches. But it seems natural. Keeps me going." He slipped off his sunglasses and winked. "You, on the other hand, would make lemons out of lemonade."

Her chin shot up in a familiar gesture of pride. "I'm simply concerned about my brother."

"It may take us awhile but we'll find Jordan."

"Guess I'll have to trust you. Some." She busied herself with her planner, checking off items on one of her lists.

The highway took them north through Portland to the ship-building town of Bath, where four lanes funneled into two. Dirty snow clumped on the shady roadsides. White frame houses and steepled churches and rambling farmhouses linked to enormous barns were sure as hell different from anywhere else he'd lived.

In Rockland, they found the fish buyer, but *Sea*

Worthy had already come and gone.

"No message neither," said the man slinging ice over bulging-eyed fish in plastic bins. "Funny thing, though. You're the second folks today to ask 'bout that Finny fella."

Rick lasered to attention. "Who were the others?"

The man shrugged. "Never give their names. Dark, foreign guys with accents. Left a couple hours ago."

"Any idea where they were headed?"

"Didn't say." The man returned to icing down the fish.

Rick thanked him and hurried a sputtering Juliana back to the truck.

"Olívas's men were here ahead of us? How did they learn about Finny?" She clicked her seat belt.

Olívas's discovery of Finny's existence reinforced his other suspicions. Later he'd call Donovan, but he didn't want to frighten Juliana more. "Wish I could answer that. Let's find your uncle."

She slashed a line through an item on her list. "That fish guy said he received no message for Finny."

"Not everyone's as organized as you. Any number of reasons the phone call didn't happen. That seemed like a loose operation. Maybe they lost the message or Finny didn't want to call, and those guys didn't want to tell you. Mayb—"

"Maybe Wes forgot to give them the message for Finny. I could telephone him." She opened her flip phone.

Shit. He was slipping. He covered her hand. "No. No calls. And turn off your phone. These days anybody can find directions for GPS tracking on the Internet. You tell anybody where we're headed?"

She startled but didn't pull away. "I . . . I had to explain part of the situation to Venice because of my cat, but I said only I had to go out of town for the day."

It would have to do.

In early afternoon, they reached the village of Bar Harbor on Mount Desert Island. They parked, then trooped to a shed at the pier's edge.

The dispatcher who worked for the boats that plied the island trade shook her head. "Beal won't return to port until tomorrow morning."

"Has anyone else been here looking for her uncle?"

"No, deah. Except for fishermen, there's no boats in the water." The woman spoke with a thick Down-East accent. "Hardly any docks."

At least the assholes hadn't arrived here ahead of them. But Rick wouldn't relax yet. The notion that somehow they knew more than they should had him gritting his teeth.

When they returned to the Silverado, Juliana directed him to her uncle's house, only a few blocks away. They found the small white Cape deserted and undisturbed.

"Locked up and the shutters are all closed," she said. "He stays here only in winter. He lives in the family's seaside cottage in warmer weather. I'm surprised he's moved already but we can try. All the property around the cottage belongs to Acadia National Park. The only access is by boat or on foot."

"Could Jordan be hiding there?"

She turned to face him, her gamine face hopeful. "I suppose, but Uncle Grady would have to help him. Provide food and such."

He turned the ignition. "Let's go. I could do with a walk after this long ride."

"Walk?" She grinned. "When I said inaccessible, I meant it. Reaching Beal Cottage is a hike, not a stroll."

At the trail's small parking area, Rick eased the Silverado behind a tangle of tall shrubs. Mostly hidden from the road, he decided. It'd have to do.

Juliana climbed into the back of the pickup to change from her jeans. He stared into the woods while counting backward from a hundred and trying not to visualize her stripping down. Having seen the hiking boots on her to-bring list, he packed his. He'd also worn a fleece pullover beneath his leather jacket, ready for temps in the thirties.

She emerged in fleece-lined jogging gear and shrugged into her backpack. She strode to the trail head, marked by a wooden sign on a pole. "We can see the cottage from the west face of Otter Mountain. We'll see smoke from the chimney if anyone is there. If not, we don't need to go farther."

He grinned at her expectant gaze. Did she have any idea how sexy she looked? Tendrils had escaped from her ponytail and curled around her face. Her eyes sparkled with the intensity he liked about her, and her complexion glowed. She worked and studied hard, like his parents when he was small, but she had too much zest for life to be called a drudge.

The trail marker described the West Face Trail as

strenuous. Towering evergreens and birches lined the steep path. "You sure you want to lug that duffel bag?"

"You have your gun?" She hooked one hand on a hip.

She had no idea how provocative that question was. He bit back a smart-ass answer and patted the holster at his back. "Always, *mi amor*, but no one followed us."

"It's not that. You have your standard equipment. So do I. You never know when we might need something I have in here."

"Let's see. A complete first-aid kit with an expandable stretcher? How about—"

"Water." She shook a finger at him. "Never go on a hike without water."

"It's your other standard equipment I appreciate more."

A flush pinked her cheeks. "Snow and ice stay until April on some of the trails. So watch your step. And it's pretty steep."

"Don't worry. I stay in shape." The warm-up pants concealed her sleek legs, but hugged other places. The view of her cute little butt would keep him going. "You first."

She checked her watch. "Right. DEA, former SEAL and all that. Okay, let's see if you can keep up. My best time on this trail is forty minutes." With that, she set out up the rocky path at a rapid clip.

- 7 -

Rick stood rooted to the spot. He stared at her disappearing backside. The woman was running up the mountain trail and timing it. He bounded after her.

The path rose straight and steep at nearly a forty-five degree angle through dense trees and undergrowth. Blue trail arrows marked boulders the size of SUV's along the way. He easily skirted the few patches of ice. By the third trail marker, he caught up to her.

"Whoa, Ms. Marathoner, what are you doing?" He tried not to sound breathless, though San Francisco was the last place he'd raced uphill. Everything there was on a damn hill.

"Hiking the trail, of course." She bent to adjust her socks. "What's the matter?"

"How can you look at the scenery if you move at mach five?"

"If you haven't noticed, we're surrounded by trees and rocks. The real scenery appears above the tree line."

"Last I knew rocks and trees *are* real scenery." He waved toward the trees. "I've traveled the globe, but I can't help the comparison to my native Miami. This is as different from palms and hibiscus as the Metropolitan Opera is from indie rock. I want to enjoy it."

Juliana glanced from the brown leaves underfoot to the cedars and naked maples and birches around them. "Sorry. I'm so used to these trails that I make it a contest with myself. It's fun trying to beat my times." Her contrite smile disarmed him.

"Always lists and numbers, Juliana." He grinned. She was unique. In more ways than one. "You'll be a hell of an accountant."

"The best views are up where the trees stop and the mountain is nothing but slabs of pink granite. Like the song says, you can see forever on a clear day. Like this one." Clearly eager to get moving again, she jogged in place. "And I might find Jordan."

"You win. We'll race up, but let's cool it on the return. Check out the trees. Listen to the birds." *Steal a few kisses.*

"It's March. Most birds are still in Miami. But it's a deal." With a pure, happy smile that rocked him, she sprinted uphill.

He raced after her. Halfway up they shed outer garments and knotted jacket sleeves at their waists. In five minutes over her previous record, they reached the end of tree cover and their destination.

The last Ice Age had scraped the mountain's heights to bedrock, endless slabs of pink and gray granite frosting on a rounded cake. The wind carried a salty tang. Scraggly bushes and stunted evergreens sprouted here and there, but nothing blocked the panorama. The view stole the remainder of his breath. He sank onto the low branch of a gnarled cedar.

From the West Face the trail led them to the south side of Otter, facing the vast indigo expanse of the Gulf of Maine. "When Dad died and the family was in turmoil, I came up here to find balance. I feel close to Heaven on this mountain."

"I see what you mean. I've always lived by the water, but I've never looked down on it this way. Not even in San Francisco, where city streets and buildings interfered."

"The cottage is just down there on the shore, white with double chimneys." She offered him binoculars, but the sag in her shoulders told him what he'd see.

Rick adjusted the focus. "No boat. No smoke from either chimney. All quiet."

She sighed and her chin trembled. "No Jordan. And Uncle Grady's still out delivering wood or windows or groceries to the islanders."

He felt her disappointment all the way to his toes. "Look at it this way. Now Olívas and company won't find him here either."

She plucked the water bottle from her backpack and offered it in exchange for the binoculars. She pointed beyond the shore. "Look out there. Those islands. That's Great Cranberry and Black and Swan."

He imagined he tasted her on the bottle's lip. He thirsted for her, not water. Her nipples puckered against her tee. She slipped on her jacket before he had to start counting again. Damn, was she trying to kill him? Temptation to the last thread of endurance.

He squinted in the general direction she'd pointed. "I can't see exactly where you're pointing."

She raised her right arm again. "This way."

He rose and stepped close behind her, circling her waist with his left arm. "This way is just fine." Bending to position his head beside hers, he slid his right hand along her pointing one. The peach fragrance of her curls tickled his senses. When he grazed his lips along the rim of her ear, she went as still as the mountain.

"Ah, now I see the islands." He tongued his way around her ear and sucked the lobe. One of her curls brushed his nose.

"Um, Rick?" Her voice came as a thready whisper.

"Mmm, *querida*?" He licked downward, along her smooth neck. At the hitch in her breath, he smiled against her skin, salty from the climb. She was warm and sweet and responsive as a blossom in the sun, and he wished it wasn't fucking March in New England and they weren't standing on a damn pile of stone.

"The scenery?" She sighed and leaned into him. As though to give him better access, she arched her neck.

"This view's fine. Closer." He nuzzled the hollow by her collarbone. "Don't you like this?"

"Oh . . . yes, but—"

"Well, then." He shouldn't. He had to. He turned her in his arms and found her mouth. The taste of her lips steamed the blood in his veins.

When she twined her arms around him and parted her lips, he hardened with a rush, intense and aching.

"Juliana." He sat on the boulder behind him and pulled her between his thighs so they were flush together. His body quivered with a need for her so intense it seared him to his soul.

He craved her like a parched man did water. He ached to dive into her and see her eyes flare with passion, feel her clench around him. Maybe that would cleanse her from his system.

He spread his left hand across her firm bottom to mold her against him. She undulated against his arousal, pressed her breasts against his chest. Angling her sideways he slipped his other hand under her shirt to cup one firm globe.

She sucked in a ragged breath and leaned into his hand.

His body pulsed with jagged need.

With one last savoring sweep of his tongue, he set her away from him. "If we don't stop now, I'll embarrass myself." He pressed a kiss to each of her palms. His hands shook as he released hers. If only he had a cigarette. "Tonight. Tonight I'll make love to you in a bed until we're both senseless, but this mountain is too hard."

If the stones beneath her feet had erupted, she couldn't have looked more shocked. Embarrassment flamed her face. "No."

"No, you don't want me to stop? You don't want to wait?" His lips twitched with a grin. "Then we can try that low branch."

She backed away, apparently too dazed to spell it out. "No . . . I mean *no*."

He understood, but reluctantly, and allowed himself a dollop of smugness at her incoherence. She wanted him.

But would he be betraying all he stood for by having sex with this woman? No. Her brother might be involved in the trafficking, but he'd bet his next paycheck on her innocence. Standing, he held up his hands. "I told you I would stop and I'm a man of my word."

"It's my fault. I shouldn't have let it get this far. My brother's welfare is my concern. I can't . . ." Her spine stiffened as she summoned composure. Averting her eyes, she repacked the water bottle and donned her jacket. "We should start down. Ready?"

"I'm always ready. Don't you know that?" Teasing was better. Laughter diluted tension. Held fear at bay. Laughter also seduced. He hoped.

"You're impossible." Her lips curved in a warm—forgiving?—smile that made his heart bump an extra beat.

After a sweep of the pink granite sloping to the woods and the distant blue water, they retraced their steps.

Juliana hopped from boulder to boulder. "How did you become a DEA Agent? Didn't your dad want you to be a doctor like him?"

"Safe subject?"

"Don't laugh at me. Really. Tell me."

He considered his answer until they reached the tree cover. "Two of my sisters are doctors. Lupe's a pediatrician, and Dolores is studying pathology. Dad wanted me to follow in his footsteps, but medicine wasn't for me."

The trail leveled through an area of switchbacks

around sheer faces of granite. The rock-strewn U-turns dropped almost as steeply. At the second switchback, a lively chattering resounded from the spruce trees.

Rick stopped her with a hand on her shoulder. "There, you hear it?" he said. "Hey, there *are* birds. What are they?" The tiny black-winged creatures darted from tree to tree.

"Chickadees. Some birds do stay here for the winter. We might see a cardinal too." Juliana adjusted her pack. "Not medicine. You wanted more adventure. Is that it?"

"Maybe. Science isn't my thing. A profession like that keeps you in school forever, ties you down." Folding his arms, he leaned against a tree.

"Why the DEA?"

"Drugs are an evil that destroys too many of my people, Cuban and other Latinos."

He paused, considering how much he wanted to reveal. He wanted her to understand—and to see the connection to Jordan. "I had a brother, Rodolfo—Rudy. Two years older. He stuck up for me when we were little. Taught me to dribble in soccer and basketball."

"You had a good relationship."

"The best. Until his teens. Rudy hung out with the club crowd, got into drugs—Ecstasy, cocaine, heroine. Addiction led to working for the drug gang. Another of El Águila's tentacles. One day Rudy disappeared into the bowels of Miami only to surface in the morgue. At age sixteen. I *have* to fight that scourge. Rid the world of El Águila's infection."

The color drained from her cheeks, and fear was

stark in her gaze. His tale had scared her, maybe too much. She cleared her throat and blinked. "That's so sad, Rick. I can't imagine how hard that would be on a family. Tell me more about your brother. What was he like?"

Why didn't make sense, but telling her was easy. "Rudy was smart and driven. He always had to be the best. Maybe that's why when he rebelled, he crashed and burned."

"Did he look like you?"

"Mostly. Taller, maybe because he was older." Rick shoved away the errant thought that he'd never know Rudy's adult height. "But he was so passionate. You could see the fire in his eyes. Me, I got by on—"

"Charm. Not that you don't have passion, mind you." She gave him a soft smile. "No wonder you're so dedicated. Your parents must be proud of you. Especially your dad."

He shrugged. *Papá* had never said as much. "I don't see him enough to know."

Her blue-green gaze perused him earnestly. She placed a hand on his arm. "It would be hard not to be bitter about that. Did you and your dad used to be closer?"

Her gentle comfort soothed the resentment he usually hid from people. "Maybe before Rudy died. Dad was only a teenager when he escaped from Cuba. He had to work hard to become a doctor. That meant a *papá* too busy for family dinners or soccer games." He understood his dad's drive, but didn't accept its cost.

"Aha."

"What's *aha* supposed to mean?"

Her full lips curved in a gentle smile. "Just that all families seem to be so complicated. Balancing numbers on a spreadsheet is way easier than adding up people. Sometimes I resent Molly racing all around searching for God knows what, and I have to remind myself she's just doing the best she knows how. Maybe that applies to your dad."

"Maybe." He watched a gray squirrel foraging in the leaves. The creature retrieved a pinecone and scurried away. Scrounging to feed the family. "My parents have done nothing their entire lives but work. I want freedom, fun in my life while I'm young."

"No ties, no responsibilities. I see." She tilted her head as if at an insight. "You miss your family though, don't you?"

"A DEA agent signs a mobility agreement. They can send us anywhere. But yes, I miss home. I miss my family."

"Moving around the country, excitement and danger, your cup of tea?" Her brows drew together in a pensive frown, and she sat on a fallen log.

"Don't forget to add paperwork, bureaucracy, and red tape to that excitement." He flopped beside her and stretched out his legs in the mulch of pine needles and dead leaves. "Someday I'd like to try for a Miami placement, a promotion. But the way this case is going, I'll be lucky to retain special agent status." He traced a vein on the back of her soft hand.

"That doesn't sound like the optimistic guy I started the day with," she said in a tight voice. Did the sensitive stroking evoke the same erotic sensations he felt?

"*¡Ay, Dios mio!* Your worrywart disease must be contagious. What shall I do?"

"Does that mean no more kisses?" Her mouth curved, but her gaze remained somber.

The possibility shook him more than he wanted to admit. If she was only teasing, he could be patient. "Hopeful or disappointed, Juliana?"

In the silence of her hesitation, the fine hairs on Rick's neck raised. Instinct switched on. What was different about the woods? He shot a comprehensive glance around.

"I—"

He covered her mouth with his fingers. "Listen," he whispered.

- 8 -

She cocked her head. When he lifted his hand, she whispered, "I don't hear anything. What is it?"

"Nothing. That's just it. The critters didn't mind our invasion, but now all is quiet." The gut-sure sense of danger switched on his experience and training.

Detach. Absorb. Analyze.

"What's wrong?" She bit her lower lip, fear in her wide eyes.

Dammit, his cop tone had frightened her rather than merely caution her. Perhaps she ought to be frightened.

"Could be nothing." Stones clattered farther down the trail below the switchbacks. He levered to his feet and held a hand on her trembling shoulder. His gut tightened. "You stay here while I scope it out."

"Have they found us? Is it El Águila's men?"

At the quavering in her voice, the screw tightened. "It might be more hikers, but I won't

74

take a chance."

"What if they hear you coming?"

He leveled a long, silent look.

"Oops, sorry." Juliana's eyebrows drew together. "I forgot you were 007."

"Bond, no, but on SEAL missions I earned the nickname The Invisible Man." He led her into the woods and behind a boulder where she'd be hidden from the path. "I'll come back in a few minutes. Stay here, and don't make any noise."

The slow tip of her head didn't reassure him.

"I mean it. Stay put." He shed his jacket and thrust it at her. He could move better without it. Quieter. He checked his SIG. Replaced the weapon in his belt holster.

Squeezing her shoulders, he planted a kiss on her forehead.

Before Juliana could protest, Rick vanished into the trees as silently and invisibly as a ribbon of smoke.

She hunched against the rock, listening. Whatever noises they heard below could come from ordinary hikers, but maybe the Mexicans were on the island.

This excitement and their chat hadn't restored her balance after that stunning embrace. She floated between frenzied desire and shimmering oblivion. He was sexy and dangerous, and she shouldn't succumb, but when he touched her, her body—and her heart—ignored all warning bells.

Maybe she'd been alone too long. Her involvement with Bill ended months ago. Then she'd had no time for a social life, much less a serious hook-up. His lovemaking never radiated desire like liquid flames through her like Rick's kisses.

Was she that vulnerable, or did the chemistry between them burn hotter than his Miami sun? Dammit, she'd rubbed against him like a cat in heat.

The more she learned about him added up to a more complex Ricardo Cruz than she'd expected. More than the smooth charmer she first thought. Including his honorable retreat when she said no.

His brother's death from drugs had fired his zeal—his hatred of drugs and those who dealt in the dirty business. No wonder he wanted *her* brother at all costs. He must think her family was dirty. Did he suspect even her? The thought had her shifting her feet.

And where was the man? He'd sneaked into the woods with a panther's stealth, evidence of his military expertise. He'd be fine.

She drummed fingers against the rough stone. She mangled her lower lip. Why didn't he come back? How long had he been gone? She stared at her watch. Five minutes? Ten?

She tied his jacket to her pack with shock cord and jogged in place. She couldn't just wait here doing nothing. She was putting off disclosing one more place Jordan might be. She *had* to reach her brother first, and she'd deceive Rick if she had to. To balance accounts, she might be able to help him now. She adjusted her pack and tiptoed into the trees.

The scent of pine and the sweetish decay of leaves mingled in the cold air. She concentrated on her surroundings, listening for voices or footsteps as she tried to follow Rick's path. The only sounds came from branches clicking together in the breeze.

And her clattering heart.

Grasping trees and rocks for support and avoiding the sparse undergrowth and patches of ice, she maneuvered down the steep grade. At every footfall, the terrain mocked her attempts at stealth. Twigs snapped. Pebbles clattered. Desiccated leaves shivered.

How the hell did Rick do it?

She focused on the ground and eased around an ice patch to step on a soft patch of reindeer moss. There. No sound.

The next step took her silently to a clump of bearberry, its stems devoid of summer's shiny green leaves and red berries. Grinning with success, she hopped over a jagged stone to a lichen-encrusted boulder. When an overhanging branch snagged her pack, the sere wood broke with a loud snap. Her breath caught in her lungs and her heart seemed to stop.

Crack! The report came from below. That was no branch.

Her stomach knotted and her temples felt clamped in a vise. She swallowed and made herself listen. Made herself think. The scrabble and thumping below meant her failure at stealth didn't matter.

She slid and leaped downhill toward the dissonance of combat. She raced through underbrush and over logs. When she rounded the boulder marking the last switchback, she crouched and peered through a tangle of branches.

A figure in dark clothing lay beneath the cedar tree at the trail's edge. A crimson stream trickled onto the frozen earth beneath his head. Needles pierced her heart.

But the clothing was wrong. Not Rick. *Thank God.*

Guttural exhalations and the jarring stridency of bone striking flesh and bone drew her gaze beyond the wounded man. Rick and the man she'd dubbed Droopy Mustache grappled in the middle of the steep trail. They struggled for possession of the pistol in Rick's right hand. Another pistol lay in the middle of the rocky path.

Heart pounding against her sternum, she bit her lower lip. If she rushed out and grabbed the discarded pistol, then what?

Mustache delivered a chop to Rick's right arm. Rick's pistol sailed across the rocks like a pebble skimming water. When he tried to dive for it, Mustache wrenched his arm.

From her downhill side came the scrabble of someone on the gravel path. She hunkered lower in the underbrush.

It was the other one, the heavy-set, lumpish one who had pinned her for Droopy Mustache's interrogation. Lumpy halted beside his prostrate comrade, but barely spared him a glance, his attention focused on the fight. The man presented his back to her, but held a pistol with a long black barrel.

She had to stop him. She shrugged off the pack and searched it for a possible weapon. Lumpy was short and built like a bulldog, but maybe . . .

Mustache twisted, holding Rick in a headlock. Lumpy stepped toward the combatants.

A spasm gripped her chest. She slapped a hand

over her mouth to contain a scream. She crept out, planting each step with precision. *Don't let him turn around.*

Lumpy stared ahead. He didn't notice her stealing closer.

Rick jerked away and shot an elbow hard into Mustache's belly. Freed, Rick spun and snaked out a sideways kick that knocked his opponent flat.

Lumpy aimed the pistol.

Juliana brought the binoculars down on his head with so much force she nearly fell over. The plastic cracked like a champagne magnum on a ship's bow.

Lumpy dropped like a lightning-struck tree. He didn't move.

She stood dazed. Her breath came in great gulps. The busted binoculars slipped from her shaking hands to the ground.

Rick glared at her, eyes blazing black fire. "What the hell are you doing here? I told you—" He dragged in a breath and shook his head. Pistol in hand, he hoisted Mustache up and then marched him over to lie with his cohorts. He grabbed the other guns and checked them before tucking them in his waistband.

"Are you all right?"

She nodded and gaped at him. Blood and dirt daubed his left cheek. A gouge disfigured his jaw and blood smeared his lower lip. His sleeve was torn. "You're hurt."

"Just a few scrapes."

She clenched her jaw and banished the dizziness, willing her pulse to calm. They weren't out of this yet. "Those two accosted me in Portland."

Lumpy moaned and clutched his head. The other

man opened his eyes. The wound was on his shoulder, but the blood had flowed downhill toward his head.

"They have a lot more than that to answer for." His brows furrowed. "And I have nothing to tie their hands with."

She was usually prepared for any emergency, but her experience had until recently consisted of computer glitches or car trouble or Jordan's rent. Having three thugs bleeding at her feet didn't fall into neat columns on a spreadsheet. Maybe she had something.

She retrieved her backpack from behind the bushes and dove into it. "Here, you can bind their hands with this." She held out a roll of duct tape.

"Pink tape?" He hooted. "I'll never again tease you about that pack."

She helped him tear off lengths of the tape and wrap them around their captives' wrists and ankles. With their attackers safely trussed, he slid his pistol into the holster.

"None of them is Olívas?" Juliana handed him his jacket.

He shook his head. "But it's a good catch. I came up behind them with my weapon drawn but one of them fired." He pointed to the first wounded man. "When this one went down, Gomez dropped his gun. Then I slipped on ice and he jumped me. That's when you came to my rescue."

He wrapped her in his arms. "*Mi brava.* My heroine. I should yell at you for not staying put. You could have been hurt."

"I heard the fight. You could have been killed." She clutched him. Oh God, he meant more to her than a means to an end. How much more she wasn't ready to examine.

Standing on tiptoe, she kissed him, her lips gentle on his injured lip. For an eternity of seconds, the cold, dangerous world disappeared. He smelled of the forest floor and sunshine and sweat, and the taste of his blood reminded her again of his human vulnerability. A hot stab of desire sliced through her, and she knew she was in trouble.

"The tape and the binocs were ingenious," he said, "but now we have to march these guys down the mountain. I need back-up to bring them in. Since I left the cell phone in the Silverado, you get your chance to race ahead."

"To call the police." She extricated herself from his embrace.

Rick handed her the keys to the truck. He arched a brow at their rapt audience. "Hurry. I don't want these sons of bitches getting too comfortable lying around on this soft mountain."

The question that had been bouncing around in her brain since he'd first detected the intruders' presence wouldn't contain itself any longer. "Rick, how did they find us? Did they know about the cottage?"

"*Querida*, either one could be the million-dollar question."

In short order, Juliana sprinted down the mountain. She had difficulty convincing the Bar Harbor Police that her tale wasn't a prank, but finally the sergeant, a friend of her uncle's, came on the line. After forty-five minutes, three police cruisers converged on the parking area.

Once in custody at the police station, the three

Mexicans lawyered up, in police jargon, and wouldn't say a word in any language. Rick arranged for federal marshals to transport the suspects to the Cumberland County Jail.

Juliana gave her story to one of the officers while Rick cleaned up in the restroom. When he returned, cleaner but still bruised, she couldn't help listening in on his phone conversation with his office.

A dark scowl knitting his brows, he stabbed a hand into the air. "How the hell did they know where to go, Jake?" He listened for a minute, then grunted a response. "I have another lead, but I'll tell you when I get back." He replaced the receiver.

"What is it, Rick? Did the other agent tell you how they followed us?"

He tunneled fingers through his hair. His burnished skin stretched taut across his high cheekbones in a fierce, hawkish expression. "Only a suspicion."

Soon they left the police station and Rick drove south. He noted Juliana's silent stare ahead into the darkness. The road stretched ahead nearly deserted and quiet, but at every turn of their search, more danger loomed for her. They were no closer to finding her brother.

If those bastards had grabbed her, her courage wouldn't have made an ice cube's difference in hell to those three. He gritted his teeth until his jaw hurt.

Once someone spilled their route to Olívas, he must have sent his men on their trail. They knew some but not all of their stops. Winter on Mount Desert Island traffic was sparse, and Rick would have spotted them. The scumbags couldn't have known about the remote cottage, so they probably checked out all the parking spots along Route 3 and got lucky.

Olívas must be getting desperate to find Jordan. What did the kid have or what did he know that was so important?

She protected her brother with all the ferocity of a mama bear. Like Rudi had defended him against bullies bent on taking his baseball mitt. She was still sticking up for her little brother against the bullies. And that included the DEA as well as the drug gang. He'd have to find out why she distrusted law enforcement so much. But wielding only a pair of binoculars, she'd defended *him*. She was a hell of a woman.

After a dinner of crab enchiladas and stuffed zucchini at The Mex in Ellsworth, they drove south in silence. Halfway down the interstate, Juliana fell asleep. Maybe she felt more secure with him. He drove on, smiling.

Late that night, as they walked toward her apartment, Juliana said, "I hate that we have nothing in the plus column. You have those three guys in jail, and they will tell us zip."

Rick mused that she hit the mark. "We'll see who hired their shyster lawyer. Maybe that will lead somewhere."

She grinned, green eyes flashing with merriment. "You can't help seeing that silver lining, can you?"

"Being hopeful is just my nature." He started to make a smart-ass comment about striking out with her, but stopped himself. "About most things."

When Juliana stabbed her key into the door lock,

Rick saw puzzlement on her brow and tension in her shoulders. "What?"

"I know I left the deadbolt on. It's unlocked now." Her hand wavered above the knob.

- 9 -

Juliana wrapped her arms around her waist. She looked to Rick.

"Shit." He moved her to one side of the door and then flicked loose the strap holding his SIG in the holster. "Maybe Venice left it off when she fed the cat."

She whispered, "We talked about the deadbolt. Because of the break-in, you know. I even gave her a to-do list."

"Of course you did. But it could be Olívas in there." He turned the handle and flung the door wide, against the inside wall. His pistol in a two-handed grip, he stalked in low and swept the room.

Juliana remained frozen, glued against the wall. Adrenaline roared in her ears.

Smiling, Rick stowed his gun and stepped inside. "You can come in. It's all right."

She slipped to his side, mincing ahead until she saw who stepped from the bedroom.

Venice Aaron wielded a sling-back high heel high

over her head. In her other arm she carried the cat. Speedy opened one amber eye and yawned. She gaped in astonishment. "Detective, sugar, you sure do know how to make an entrance."

She deposited the cat on the floor and picked up the other shoe, letting both dangle from one hand. She smoothed her short flowered skirt.

"Looking mighty fine, Ms. Aaron." He grinned.

Juliana sagged against him. She dragged in a needed breath. Behind her, the door closed with a soft click. "Venice, I thought . . . we thought . . . it was the deadbolt—"

"Sorry I gave you a scare. I had me a late date. When I came home, I saw this place was dark, so I let myself in to make sure Speedy was all right. You slammin' in, I thought it was those creeps after you."

"We scared you too. I'm sorry." Juliana crossed to her friend and they hugged as Speedy wound back and forth, rubbing against their legs.

Venice held her at arm's length. "You find any trace of Jordan?"

How much could they could tell Venice? Juliana cast Rick a stricken look.

"We've had leads, but none has panned out." He strode to the window and peered out.

"Uh, huh. Leads. That's what you've been chasing." Venice leaned against a kitchen stool as she stepped into her heels. "I see things are in good—" she paused, batting her lashes at Rick "—hands. I'll leave you all alone."

"Don't go on my account." Rick reached for the door handle. "I'm leaving. Reports to do before I hit the sack."

Juliana hurried to see him out. She wanted him to go but she didn't. In spite of her protests up on the mountain, she wanted him, this Zorro in his charcoal shirt and black jeans. She was as much a fool as her brother.

He turned a shuttered expression to her before his mask fell away. He surveyed her, his gaze full of concern and awareness.

Heat shimmered between them. She forced herself not to step into his arms.

"The agent I called for earlier just pulled up outside. You'll be covered now. Safe." He stepped closer and tucked a stray curl behind her ear. Her skin tingled where his finger rasped its trail. His minted breath brushed her skin. He gave her a wistful smile."

When Rick was gone, Venice scooted up onto the kitchen stool. "That man looked like he was gonna spend the night. Hope I didn't scare him off."

Juliana choked on her friend's too-perceptive assumption. Speedy's amber gaze reflected her confusion. Neither one knew what was going on. She lifted him from the floor and sat on the other stool with him purring in her lap. "You're imagining things. There's nothing between us."

"Could've fooled me." Venice scratched the cat's chin. "His sexy dark eyes never left you. And his heart was in them. You can't look at emotions like numbers on a balance sheet. Tell me you don't think for a minute he's a user like your mother's con men."

"I know that, but I'm not sure he does."

"I'm no rose-colored glasses kind of girl. My

mama named her baby girl for a city that's sinking into the sea. But I know it does no good to sit around fretting like a cat in the rain. If you want that man, grab him."

"I have no time for romance . . . or a hook-up. Until Jordan's safe, he's my priority."

"Girlfriend, there's only so much you can do about this fix Jordan's gotten himself into. Let the cops handle things. If you have a chance for some happiness, go for the gold."

Juliana doubted there was any future past a few passionate nights. She shook her head, trying to shake some sense into her tired brain.

During the next few days, Rick worked from a desk in the Portland DEA office. He fought the urge to drive to Portsmouth to see Juliana. To wrap himself in her scent, to feel her soft skin, to drown in her eyes. Damn.

Instead, he harassed the guys assigned to protect her, checked on them every other hour, generally provoking them to the brink of violence.

The next Monday, Juliana had her car back. An agent followed her to and from work at Vinson Seafood. If she was keeping something from him, she'd made no moves to indicate that. No moves one way or another. She was safe. That's all he should care about. She was a woman he should avoid. And he wasn't the man she needed.

He buried himself in the El Águila files. His percolating investigative instincts kept brewing up Wesley Vinson as the American connection, but so far he didn't have enough for a search warrant. No evidence. No witnesses.

The draggers, 120-foot-long boats that netted bottom fish like haddock and flounder, seemed in the clear. They chugged into port after nine or ten days at sea, then steamed out to fish again. With crews of six or more, keeping drug smuggling under wraps would be as hard as maintaining a secret in his gossipy family.

Purse seiners, eighty-foot boats with smaller crews. More possibility. Motoring out every day in search of bait fish like herring, a captain could easily meet another boat at sea and add a package or two to the cargo. The Coast Guard couldn't be everywhere at once. They would pay no special heed. Even if Rick had the schedules and cargo lists and checked them against the DEA's list of intercepted shipments, he'd still have no evidence.

The jailbirds sullenly refused to open up. More scared of their Mexican boss than of cops or prison.

He had no leads on the possible leak in the Boston office either. The notion of betrayal roiled in his gut. Same tangled emotions Juliana probably felt about Jordan. Hell.

His only hope was in the *Sea Worthy*'s return to Portland in another week. Finnegan Farnham would have to answer a lot of questions. A fast run in a Coast Guard cutter might get some quick answers, but it would also send up warning signals to the smugglers so they could scurry back under their rocks.

Too much frustration for even a patient man.

On Tuesday, an Oxford County sheriff's deputy found Sudsy Pettit's truck abandoned in the woods. Rick spent the rest of the day at the scene and at the state medical examiner's building in Augusta. On Wednesday, hoping to see Juliana before she left for work, he headed to her apartment.

As he left the interstate at the Portsmouth exit, his cell phone sang out.

It was the Portland-based agent in charge of Juliana's guard duty. "Something odd going on here," the agent said. "Ms. Paris just left in her foxy neighbor's Honda SUV. License plate CANALBT. She's wearing a long black wig."

Shock vibrated like a wire along Rick's arms. He fisted his hand on the steering wheel. He'd been right. Juliana was hiding something. Or someone— her brother. He forced his fingers to unclench as he pushed aside the emotions knocking around inside him.

"Thanks for the heads-up. I'll take it from here."

Juliana fiddled with the defroster and headlights. Too bad Venice's generosity with her SUV didn't come with dashboard lessons. There, finally the fog lights came on. Amorphous knots of white hovered over the street and wound around the trash bins like ghostly curtains.

She usually hated New England's murky weather but today the cottony fog and the fine drizzle that concealed her were perfect. Nothing could suppress the guilt riding her at sneaking away like this, but the opportunity was too good to pass up.

Involving Venice and leaving her with the old Sentra weren't her best decisions but what else could she do? Ransoming the car from Ray's Recks took nearly every cent she made in the last week.

The fact that she and Ray went to high school together didn't soften his policy on paying the deductible up front.

She turned onto Woodbury Avenue and headed for I-95. The headlights flashed on a parked car facing her. A familiar tall figure emerged from the dark sedan. The collar of his jacket turned up, Ricardo Cruz strode to the middle of the street.

Busted, dammit. Her stomach bucked and rolled, but whether from panic or elation at seeing him again, she couldn't tell. The damn man was just standing there, daring her to drive into him. She stomped on the brakes.

Rick stalked to the driver side window. A fine drizzle glistened on the leather jacket and dripped from his hair. From the expression on his face, she expected to see steam rising. He arched a brow and circled an index finger.

Resigned, she pushed the button to lower the window.

A car honked and sped around them. The driver shot them the bird.

"A little early for Halloween." Rick tugged on a lock of hair that had escaped the wig's tight net.

Her face went hot and a frisson hummed through her. She yanked off the wig and tossed it in the back. "I . . . need some time on my own. I'm tired of being followed and escorted everywhere."

"Ah. Then I won't follow you. Unlock the passenger door, Juliana."

Little choice there. If she drove off, he'd just follow her or send another agent after her. She hit the unlock button with more force than necessary. "Be my guest."

When he jumped inside, her greedy gaze devoured the sight of him—coal-black hair gleaming wet, face rugged and tight with anger. He smelled of rain and leather and she wanted to slide across the console and into his arms. She gritted her teeth.

He settled into the seat. "You know where Jordan is? Did he phone you?"

"You'd know if he had. You people monitor all my calls."

A pickup came up behind her, so she accelerated.

Rick stretched out his long legs and placed his left hand on her seat back, casual, as if they were going on a date. Only a muscle flexing in his jaw betrayed his tension.

Maybe she'd drive around aimlessly and he'd get tired of his game. Except this was no game. If she could find Jordan, he could answer so many questions. If only she understood his involvement with the drug gang. If he knew what that truck was hauling or at least suspected. If he had an idea why the drug gang was so desperate to find him.

The camp was her last chance, the last place to look for Jordan. He *had* to be there. Was it betrayal if she turned over her brother to a DEA agent? Decision time. She had to follow her heart and her instincts and trust Rick. But the thought was a lump in her throat.

When she took the northbound ramp on the interstate, he asked, "Where are we going?"

"The Lakes Region of Maine. The family has a cabin on Crooked Lake. It's the last place I know to look for my brother." She hiked her shoulders in a gesture of helplessness. Matters were definitely out of her control.

"So that's the secret you've been keeping. Your family sure has the hideaways."

"Uncle Grady's on my dad's side of the family. Crooked Lake is Mom's family. You may think it's strange, but lots of Maine families have hunting and fishing and summer camps." Now why did she feel she had to defend the entire state of Maine?

"Don't you have to work today?"

"Venice called in sick for me. Enough people there have had a bug that no one will question my excuse. Vinson will call for another temp." She slanted a look at him. No muscle twitching. Maybe his calmed temper would transfer to Jordan. "And you? What about that car you left in Portsmouth?"

"Another agent will pick it up. No problem."

"I was planning to spend the night."

"I'm good with that."

Whatever he meant by that, she wasn't ready to examine.

As the car sped northward, they fell into an almost companionable silence. North of Portland, they left the interstate and the wet weather behind. The SUV rolled onto two-lane country roads and into bright sunshine.

She hummed with awareness of the man beside her. Realization pummeled her. Rick possessed more depth and honor than Molly's shallow Good-time Charlies, but commitment and security weren't in his vocabulary. Life was more vivid, more intense with him. In spite of all her efforts at guarding her heart, she'd fallen in love with him. With his laughter, with his gentleness and strength, and with the poetry in his eyes.

With a man who'd break her heart.

Rick's fingers itched to caress Juliana's penny-bright curls, freed from the fright wig and loosely bound atop her head. She wore dark purple jeans, but the parka concealed what else, maybe the matching sweater he liked. She focused on traffic and the maze of roads with the same fierce concentration she did everything.

He wanted that fierce passion focused on him, wanted her beyond all reason. And hell, how could he stay angry with her for doing what he'd have done for his brother? She could've kept up the deception and taken them sightseeing around the Granite State. Instead she yielded to his accompanying her, to the inevitable. Finally she was seeing reason.

A secluded cabin? He almost let himself hope Jordan was hiding somewhere else.

"The cabin, Juliana, tell me about the cabin." Adjusting for the sudden tightness in his jeans, he shifted in the bucket seat.

"Just a hunting and fishing camp, really." A nibble on her lower lip betrayed her anxiety. "Pretty basic. It's on paper company land. My grandfather built the cabin back in the forties. Another relative pays the rent."

A cabin on timber land. No title. No wonder a search of assets didn't turn that up. He watched the scenery, ready to see what developed.

They stopped for clam chowder at The Galley in Naples. When they returned to the SUV, he grasped her arm. "Don't start the engine just yet. I have news but I didn't want to tell you inside or while you were driving."

She looked stricken. "Jordan?"

He smiled to ease her worry. "See, that's the reaction I thought might take us off the highway. No, it's about the guy he was driving for. A sheriff's deputy found Sudsy Pettit's truck in the woods near Norway. Two dead bodies inside. Sudsy and an unidentified male in his twenties. Dark hair, chunky."

She laid her head on the steering wheel and inhaled deeply. "Thank God. Jordan's blond and wiry."

"I wanted to tell you this in person. The reason I was headed to your apartment. And then the agent guarding you phoned me."

"*Unidentified male,*" she repeated, giving him a watery smile. "Because I'd have thought it was Jordan."

"Exactly. Both men died from a single shot to the back of the head. Execution style. If Jordan's in the cabin, you better hope he's ready to turn himself in."

"I'll make sure he understands." But she looked doubtful.

Close to the turnoff for Crooked Lake, they bought food at a tiny village store. Ten miles of gravel road led in to the lake. From the road, a narrow dirt track plunged downhill to the small log cabin.

He searched among the bare birches. "No power lines. Are they underground?"

"No electricity. It's only a sporting camp. No plumbing either. The only running water's a hand pump in the kitchen sink." Her features tightened. "Is that a problem?"

"Don't look so stricken." He smiled. With a forefinger, he smoothed the worry lines that popped out on her forehead. "It's fine."

"No cell phone towers, no internet connection of any kind."

No problem for his satellite phone. "I'll deal."

Juliana guided the vehicle down the bumpy drive. "Mud season's only begun to thaw the ground, so the driveway's not too bad. But this hill needs four-wheel drive any time of year, or you might end up in the front door. Or in the lake."

She eased to a stop beside a small outbuilding and they got out.

Judging from the lack of footprints in the patchy snow and the smokeless chimney, no one had used the camp all winter. Including Jordan.

Warmth suffused him, swirling in his belly like one of Juliana's butterflies. As much as he needed to find her brother, Jordan's presence would have inhibited what Rick knew would happen, wanted to happen, *needed* to happen, between him and Juliana.

"By the water," he said in a mild tone. "Not a bad hideout. Too bad he's not here."

Disappointment was stark in her eyes, but she rallied, straightening her shoulders. "I refuse to feel guilty for not telling you everything. I'm entitled to protect my brother. I told you from the beginning I intended to talk to him first."

"And yet you've brought me although you suspected Jordan was here. Does that mean you've had a change of heart about him?" He looked down at his boots and then up at her. "Or about me?"

NEVER SURRENDER

- 10 -

Not ready to answer what he was really asking, Juliana turned away.

She unlocked the padlock on the plank door and opened it. "It'll feel colder inside than out. We'll need a fire in the Franklin."

"I'll take care of that if you have other things to do." He set their purchases on the kitchen counter and went out to the woodpile.

In the downstairs bedroom she sank onto the bed and put her head in her hands. Her chest ached and tears burned her eyes. Nowhere else to look. No way to contact Jordan. *Dammit, where are you, little brother?* He had to be safe, tucked away somewhere no bad guys could find him. Even if she came up with an idea, she could do nothing now. She wiped her eyes with a tissue and pushed to her feet.

She exchanged her good jeans and ballet flats for old jeans and sneakers. She pulled curtains open, swept sheets from the two rocking chairs and Naugahyde sofa, and shook mouse droppings from the rag rugs.

What would Rick think of the place? The entire cabin took no more space than a two-car garage, with one large room for sitting and cooking, a bedroom downstairs with a queen bed, and a loft with bunks. Sets of deer antlers and mounted fish adorned the walls. Driftwood and carved lamps completed the woodsy décor. A path led to the outhouse.

It couldn't compare well to anything he was used to. Houses in Florida must be light and airy and open, not dumpy and dreary like this old cabin.

"Cozy." Rick entered with an armload of birch logs. "I love to watch a fire." His mouth curved with boyish enthusiasm.

She puffed out a sigh and returned his smile. He'd removed his leather jacket. The wood's weight stretched the shirt across his muscled shoulders as he arranged the logs in the hearthside box. His hair gathered highlights from the sunshine streaming in the window.

Her heart rioted against her ribs. She longed to caress the high slope of his cheek, the bristly sweep of his jaw. Instead, she hurried to the SUV for the foam cooler.

She wouldn't reject him this time, but she wasn't ready. Yet. Loving him confused her. Desire swirled with anxiety and fear. She'd deceived him, except he found her out. And since Jordan wasn't here, she might have to deceive him again.

"The lake, the cabin—it's something from a post card," he said when she returned. "I've bivouacked in tents and on hard and soggy ground, but never in an honest-to-God log cabin."

His admiring tone of voice said he was enjoying himself in spite of his reason for coming. That eager joy in life had endeared him to her from the beginning. He made everything special, made being with him special.

"We can light the fire later." She zipped her parka. "It's turned into a beautiful day. Why don't we go for a hike? Melting ice is too punky for snowmobiling or ice fishing."

From a hook by the door, she tossed him an old barn coat of her dad's.

"No racing. I want to savor every bit of this place, the lake, the clean air." He slid a finger down her forehead to the tip of her nose. "You."

"Absolutely. No competition." She deliberately ignored the tingle his touch ignited. She unclipped her barrette and smoothed her hair.

Before she could clamp it again, he plucked up the barrette. He let a handful of hair run through his fingers. "This is beautiful, like a sunset halo. Leave it loose, *querida*." He tucked the clasp into her coat pocket. "For me."

Mesmerized by his poetry and his musky scent, layered with mint, Juliana could only bob her head like a mechanical toy. Before he could kiss her, she ducked out the door.

She traipsed to the water's edge. Mushy ice covered most of the center, but at the shore, the clear water lapped gently against a narrow cobble beach. She picked up a rock. "Does skipping stones come under the heading of competition?"

"You're talking to the stone-skipping champ of South Beach." Rick hefted a small, flat rock. "This'll be a snap. You don't have the water hazards we do in Florida."

From the devilment gleaming in his eyes, she should have known not to bite, but she couldn't help it. "Water hazards?"

"Alligators."

Laughter bubbled up. She didn't believe his wild tale, but she'd play along. "Alligators. I'd like to see that. What do you do, try to skip off its head?"

"I'm crushed, Juliana. I get the feeling you don't believe me." His grin faded, his dark brows beetling in a severe expression she couldn't interpret. "No, the game is to avoid the alligator. Best not to rouse him. The beasts are unpredictable."

"So you hope you have a body of water without an alligator. Much safer that way."

"Even if you don't see one, the possibility injects tension into the game."

Were they still discussing alligators? Or maybe she was reading too much into a playful conversation. She averted her gaze to search for a flat stone.

"Let's see what I can do with these Maine rocks." One smooth swing sent his stone skimming the water. Three skips and it sank with a plop. "Out of practice."

"No alligators." Eyeing the glittering surface, she curved her fingers around her skipper, smooth and gray as rain. With a snap, she sent it flying.

One, two, three, four hops before it thudded onto an ice raft.

"Not bad. Without the ice, you might have gotten another bounce or two." He stepped in front of her. "You want to teach me your technique? You could guide my swing. Come wrap your arms around me."

"You are such a hound." Laughing, she pushed a stone into his hand. "I'm not falling for that. And I'm not showing you any tricks. You have quite enough of your own."

After a lengthy competition, which Rick declared a tie but Juliana insisted she won, they trekked around Crooked Lake. Bare maples and birches interspersed with spruce and other evergreens ringed the angular body of water. At irregular intervals, cottages loomed in the woods, dark and boarded up.

His appreciation of this remote spot was contagious. With him at her side, the crisp air seemed sweeter and sharper, permeated with the tangy scent of the surrounding firs.

By the time they returned to the cabin, shadows stitched over the sun diamonds on the lake surface. He lit the Coleman lantern hanging in the small kitchen and she laid a fire in the Franklin.

She sorted through the groceries. "Chicken, green pepper, onion, rice, garlic. "Mmm, I can't wait to taste this Cuban culinary creation you've been promising me. I looked it up."

"Of course you did."

"*Arroz con* polo, is that how you say it?"

"*Pollo*." He pronounced it *poyo*. "Won't be authentic without the saffron, but it'll do."

"*Arroz con pollo* sounds exotic. Does it mean something glamorous?"

He ambled closer, his rich laughter echoing against the log rafters and down her spine. "If you think 'rice with chicken' is glamorous."

She wrinkled her nose. "Glamorous doesn't

matter, but tasty does. Do you have the recipe?"

"You probably want it in a list to get it exact." He caught her to him and brushed a kiss on her mouth. "A little of this, a little of that, I can prepare this dish with my eyes closed."

She wanted to snuggle in his arms, but recipes should be measured. "But—"

"Relax. You'll see." He peered at the bottle of generic white wine she'd extracted from the shopping bag. "Too bad we have wine instead of rum. A mojito, now there's a real drink, rum and limejuice. Sitting by a fire, you'd love it."

"You keep promising me Cuban delights. When will you deliver?" Uh oh, double entendre. She was in trouble. Strangely, the prospect didn't bother her.

His eyes darkened. His long-fingered hands molded her shoulders, then slid down her spine. "When you're ready, Juliana, we'll discover our delights together."

His smooth voice flowed through her, intoxicating as a mojito. He released her. "I want nothing more than to demonstrate. Keep that thought. It's a little chilly in here for what I have in mind."

He knelt by the woodstove and added wood to the fire.

After the fire was blazing, Rick rolled up his shirtsleeves and joined Juliana in the kitchen. She chopped onions and peppers while he prepared the chicken pieces. When the chicken and vegetables were bubbling, he started the rice.

She set their places on a low pine table near the

fire.

The Franklin stove's doors stood open to display the flames, still bright behind its screen. She'd left her hair loose, and the red-gold curls seemed alive with the dancing flames. A faint smile curved her mobile mouth, drawing him to stare at her lower lip and the arched bow of the upper. This view of her gilded with firelight stirred him to rampant life.

No matter how crazy he was for her, it was still a casual relationship. And he meant to keep it that way. But casual didn't mean hands off.

He turned off the flame beneath the rice. He edged closer to her and hooked an arm around her, kissing the skin beneath her ear. Her jaw and velvety cheek lured his lips like magnets. "I could get used to this place. And the company."

She turned in his arms to flash a smile. For a change, not cautious with him, her gaze held desire. "Some families spend the entire summer here. And drive long distances to work."

"Must be nice to get away totally." He glided the back of one hand along her cheek and down her neck.

The lushness of her breasts pressed against him as she snuggled nearer. He held her, acutely aware of the length of their bodies touching—thighs and knees, hips and torsos. He sensed a similar awareness in her. This dynamo who was never still stood quietly in his arms. He nuzzled her hair and inhaled her scent.

She felt so perfect he didn't want to move. Except lust shot through him with a furnace blast. He burned for her, ached for this intriguing woman made of stubbornness and loyalty, vulnerability and humor, reserve and sensuality.

"Juliana?" Shit, you'd think he was a horny kid, a desperate one.

She gazed up at him with dreamy eyes. "Mmm? Are you hungry? You're the chef."

"I'm hungry, yes, starving—but for you." He covered her hand where it lay on his chest and laced his fingers with hers. Soft and delicate.

Her breath hitched. "Dinner will keep?"

"It'll taste even better later. Since we met I've longed to make love to you."

She sighed. "I want you too."

"And you understand—"

She placed a finger on his lips to silence him. "Shh, don't chill this evening with cold lake water. I know what I'm doing." Her smooth finger trailed across his lips.

"You won't be sorry." He captured her hand and kissed each finger. Her eyelashes drifted lower as he pushed up her sleeve and kissed his way up her arm.

Almost moaning with relief, he kissed the unbearably tender spot inside her elbow. He wanted her so much he trembled. "Tell me, Juliana, tell me what you want."

Her chin lifted, and her lashes. Desire burned with green fire in the depths of her eyes, as if alight from within. A mischievous smile tilted her mouth. "You're so romantic and poetic, but you're forcing me to be clear, so I have a list."

"A list. I can't wait."

"First, I want to be naked with you."

Flames ignited in his veins. "Juliana—"

Her cool finger on his lips silenced him. "Two, I want you to kiss me all over."

He ached at the image.

That cool finger swept sparks across his forehead and his temple. "Three, I want to explore your body as well."

"Is there a four?" *I'll die if there isn't.*

"Four, most of all, I want you inside me for what I suspect will be incredible, mind-blowing sex." She trailed a sizzling fuse down his chest to his navel.

His heart raced, and he had to clasp her shoulders to stop his hands from shaking. "I want to take it slowly with you. I want a leisurely journey of anticipation, but you make restraint impossible. I crave you so much I burn hotter than that fire."

With a smile as seductive as Eve's, she took his hand and started toward the bedroom.

"Not in there. I want to see you bathed in firelight." He rushed past her to snatch a quilt from the foot of the bed. She shoved back the sofa. He spread the quilt before the Franklin stove, then tugged her down with him onto the padded softness.

They knelt, their bodies aligned, and kissed. The heat of her mouth made him groggy with craving. With a sweep of his tongue, he probed her texture, the ridges of her teeth, the sweetness of her desire as her tongue sought his.

"We have on too many clothes."

"Agreed." She flicked open his top shirt button, then the next, and the next until she slid the garment down and off. "This shirt looks good on you. And off you."

Her fingers fumbled with his belt buckle, but he brushed them away. "Later. My turn." He peeled off her sweater, and then the lace bra. "Yeah, oh, yeah."

A blush spread over her cheeks and down to her breasts. He had to see where the rosy color would end. She sucked in a breath when he stroked a nipple.

"Beautiful. Satiny nipples the color of pink hibiscus blossoms."

She chuckled. "A breast connoisseur."

"You bet." He lowered her to their bedding and brushed his lips over each peaked nipple, laving and tasting the sweetness of her skin. When he suckled her, she arched upward and uttered a soft *ah*. He kissed down to her flat stomach. "Breast connoisseur, belly connoisseur. Any part you have with this soft skin."

A reflection of flames gilded her moistened breasts. Dizziness pulsed in his head, in his loins. His need for her overwhelmed him.

She must have seen the heat in his eyes because she unzipped her jeans and pushed them and her panties down and kicked them off. Those runner's killer legs. His gaze riveted on the curls at their apex. A darker gold, they hinted at the heated passion inside her.

That she trusted him enough to bare herself to him touched him more deeply than her desire for him. He was used to women desiring him, but trust had never been an issue. Juliana had journeyed from fearing his intentions to reliance on his skills and honor, and finally to trust. In spite of what still stood between them, she opened herself to him.

It humbled him.

The fire crackled as sap bubbled within. The flames danced and weaved, caressing each other. The only other sound was the thudding of their hearts.

He skinned away the rest of his clothing so fast that she laughed.

Before tossing away his jeans, he extracted a foil packet. "That little store might not have much of a spice and wine selection, but they had plenty of these."

"Kiss me."

He did.

At last they were skin to skin. He kissed her shoulder, her breasts, her hips and thighs and inhaled the female musk of her skin. He stroked her body as she moved beneath him.

Her hands caressed his skin, traced the contours of his muscles, and rubbed his nipples until he ground his teeth. She ran her palms down his back to his buttocks and scraped her nails over the base of his spine.

Wildfire streaking over his body, he groaned. Dammit, he would hold out long enough for her. He massaged the wet silk between her legs. "You're so ready for me."

Moaning, she reached for him, cupping him and stroking him. *"Now, Rick, now."*

When they joined, he groaned at the exquisite sensation. She was slick and small and tight. His climax clawed at him, but he took care to join them slowly, and the wonder of it, the joy of the soul-deep oneness he felt with her stilled him. Stunned him. Awed him.

She locked her legs around him, and they kissed endlessly as passion built.

He stiffened, fire surging in his blood, poised on the edge, straining to hold back until she joined him.

"Come with me, *mi mariposa*, fly with me."

And then she cried out, her strong legs gripping him as her body rippled beneath him.

Her spasms squeezed him, sent him flying with her. *"Ah . . . mi corazón, mi corazón."*

- 11 -

Two hours later, Juliana's mind and body still hummed from their lovemaking. Mind-blowing didn't begin to describe the experience. Softness uncurled inside her at the anticipation of more.

After they'd eaten and cleared away the dishes and the rest of the Cuban chicken, they built up the fire again and snuggled on the quilt. The wood fire scent layered over the chicken aromas made her drowsy.

She wore only her brother's old tee shirt. She set down the tumbler that served as a wine goblet, then leaned against the sofa.

Clad in his boxers, Rick sprawled beside her, his head in her lap, one hand stroking her knee. He turned to nuzzle her stomach, then glanced up at her with the half grin that always melted her muscles.

"What was that you said, um . . . at the end? *'Mi cor'* something."

His grin evaporated, and he went still. His eyes

clouded with what might be panic before he grinned again. Not a convincing grin, but pasted on. "Mmm, I really don't know what I said, some Spanish endearment like darling. You can't hold a man responsible for what he says at such a moment."

She blinked at his response. Was Mr. Allergic-to-Relationships being defensive? She merely requested a translation, after all, not a declaration of love. Was what he'd said more than an endearment? She might never know.

"Of course not." She stilled and her chest tightened. After he'd eased away from her, she was still drooling over him. *Fool, fool, just like Molly.*

He sat up and kissed her. Garlic and wine mingled with his familiar, dear flavor. "I can't stay here beyond tomorrow. I need to find Jordan and stop El Águila's dirty operation."

She saw the intensity of his emotions increase with each challenge he set for himself. A complex scenario. "You aren't the only agent who can do that."

"But I'm the only one who sees how it all goes together. I shouldn't tell you, but there's a leak in the DEA office. I hate the idea of another agent being dirty." He pounded a fist into the sofa cushion.

She wanted to put her arms around him and make it all go away. "I'm not surprised there's a leak. The gang has been one step ahead or one step behind us. But why does it have to be a DEA agent? Could it be someone else in your offices?"

He jabbed a hand through his hair. "Shit, I'll call Donovan now." He went to his coat and came up with his phone.

"No cell phone coverage here, remember?"

"Satellite phone. Secure. I got this."

Juliana added wood to the fire while he talked to his fellow agent. Now she had to tell him what she'd neglected to before.

After he disconnected, he kissed her. "Thanks, Ms. Super Spy."

"Anytime. And there's another possibility."

He slanted a skeptical glance her way. "Do you know something I don't?"

"Maybe. The information about Bar Harbor could've come from Wes Vinson. The day we left for Down East, I mentioned I was going to see my uncle in Bar Harbor. I didn't remember I said it until much later."

He caressed her cheek with his knuckles. "So Vinson knew where we were. Do you have any other reason to suspect him?"

"I didn't until yesterday." Recalling her shock of discovery, she hugged her knees. She liked Wes both as a boss and a friend. She felt used and betrayed. "Since I was acting as office manager, I decided to check my brother's employment record. The computer file had only his shipping dates and social security and such. Other employee folders are in a filing cabinet. Jordan's contained an interesting note."

"Don't keep me in suspense."

"Someone had written one word on a sticky note: *Sudsy*."

He swore, a staccato burst of Spanish. He leaped to his feet and prowled the small room like a caged cat.

Edginess sharpened the high curve of his

cheekbones, lending him a predatory aspect. Halting at a window, he stared into the night and rubbed the back of his neck. He stabbed at the air with an index finger. "I've had suspicions about Vinson."

"And you didn't tell me?"

"What would I tell you? No evidence. Only my gut."

"If he sent Jordan to work for Sudsy Pettit, that meant he lied about not knowing who Jordan was," she said. "Or Pettit."

He nodded. "The connection with Pettit dumps Vinson in the middle of the drug and gun trafficking, maybe at the top."

"Any craft in Vinson's fleet could easily ferry drugs from an offshore rendezvous."

"Did you ever ask him about that call he promised to make?"

"He said he faxed them about having Finny phone me. He insisted they must have lost the fax."

"Want to bet phone records show no call, fax or otherwise, to Rockland between your visit to Vinson and our trip north? I can't check without a warrant."

"He lied." Her eyes narrowed as she grasped the implications. "If he didn't want me to find Jordan, Wes must know why Jordan had to hide. Could he have told the Mexicans about Finny?"

His gaze stark with emotion, he knelt before her and grasped her shoulders. "Your info helps confirm my theory that Vinson could be Olívas's American partner."

How the son of a respectable Portland family establishment could be the major pipeline for drugs in the Northeast was beyond her. "How do you suppose he got involved?"

"Easy money, a lot easier than the fishing business. Talk to any fisherman, any owner of a seafood business. It's getting harder to find the fish. They blame too many regulations, shorter seasons, competitors. Doesn't excuse Vinson but might explain his motives."

"He could've gotten backing to modernize, to expand," she said.

"I don't have his financial records, but rumor has it he's taken out bank loans over the past several years. Had trouble paying them back until a few years ago. Suspicion is the short cut to an influx of money could've been smuggling. The connection would explain why Olívas didn't roar out in a big power boat to grab Finny off *Sea Worthy*. Vinson couldn't afford the exposure."

"You'll need proof."

"And in a hurry. We have only a few days until the *Sea Worthy* is due back in port. Vinson knows you're looking for Finny and so is the DEA. We have to get to Finny first."

"Next week. That's not much time." She smiled. He needed her. Correction. He needed her help.

Pangs of unease dimmed the glow from their lovemaking. Rick was honorable. Maybe she could trust him to find Jordan and see that he was safe. But it was the system that failed her dad. The system killed him. *How can I trust the DEA? Anyone?*

She couldn't let doubts weigh her down like a sack of rocks. She could act, not just sit by and wait. "When I go back to work, I can try to discover more."

"No. It's too dangerous. If he suspected . . ." He got up and tossed two more logs in the stove before shutting its doors.

He returned to wrap her in his strong arms. "Enough speculation for one night. I want to devote my attention to a certain woman whose talents I haven't fully appreciated."

His voice flowed over her like a caress. His gaze, hot and hungry, met hers, and sparks flared into swirling heat. Love was a more complex emotion than she expected—warm and soft one moment, steamy and sharp the next.

"Oh, yes, Rick, appreciate me." Urgency enveloped her like a sauna.

His uninhibited passion fueled her sensuality. Her feelings for him had intensified with the heart and soul connection of their joined bodies. Their idyll would end tomorrow, and she wanted to take advantage of their time together.

He scooped her up and carried her into the small bedroom. "This time I want you in a bed. I have a feeling that after I appreciate every inch of you, we'll both need sleep."

She lowered the flame on the gas lamp until its cobalt globe cast only a hazy blue aura over the bed. He followed her down and didn't resist when she pushed him onto his back.

She stripped off her shirt and his boxers before straddling his pelvis. A calculated wriggle elicited a renewed leap of desire in his eyes.

He palmed her breasts, shooting a hot flash of sensation to her center.

She shimmied against the hot ridge beneath her bare bottom. "You're mine, Mr. Macho-SEAL-agent."

The next morning, after they made love again, Rick let Juliana doze and he stared at the ceiling.

He needed to find Jordan as much as she did. The only proof against Vinson besides catching a boat in the act would be records of drug shipments. Or weapons shipments. Without cause, no search warrant. Worse, the task force had no time for surveillance of the boats or Vinson. Cases like these sometimes took months.

With only days left, someone unofficial had to snoop in Vinson's office. Someone he wouldn't suspect. *Fuck*. He'd been protecting Juliana, and now he had to deliberately send her into danger.

If only Jordan would show up. He might know about Vinson. Maybe that was what the gang feared. No clues in the kid's apartment. Most of his stuff was packed in the duffel bag.

What had she said? *He doesn't have much. Mostly he lives on a fishing boat.*

His pulse sped. He'd kick the idea around with Holt Donovan and Jake Wescott. Nothing to tell Juliana. Not yet.

Beside him, she shifted and cuddled closer, still asleep.

A quiet intensity shimmered inside him, a mix of lust and protectiveness and other sensations he couldn't name. Shit, he'd been certain that having her would sate him, would satisfy his raw hunger. Sex was recreation. Fun. Intimate, sensual fun, no big deal.

But tonight hadn't been enough. He needed more.

She filled his spirit with her responsiveness, her

sweetness, her caring. She understood him better than anyone ever had. His need for her shocked him, his need to make love to her over and over, to bind her to him. But who was bound? The power of their lovemaking had him calling out more than a casual endearment. *Mi corazón.*

My heart.

If she had his heart, what then? How could he fall for a woman with a drug dealer in the family? Even if she disbelieved the guilt. He'd be disloyal to his own brother's memory. And he had no clue how she felt about him or what she expected from him.

His heart battered his ribs like the wings of a wild green parrot he'd once seen trapped against a window. He'd freed the frantic creature, and it had flown to freedom in the sky. Was freedom truly what his heart wanted?

They finished the *arroz con pollo* for breakfast and prepared to drive back to Portland. Rick stared out the window. The coastal rains had found their way west, dampening the ground and dampening spirits. "So you're sure you know what to do?"

"That's the third time in an hour you've asked me that. You sound like me with the dire warnings and reminders." Juliana grinned as she checked her day planner.

"Be very careful. Don't let Vinson suspect we're on to him. Don't put yourself under suspicion. If you can't get at the files, we'll figure out something else." He held out her parka.

"Believe me, you can trust me to be careful." She zipped her coat and kissed him.

"I do, *querida*, about as far as you trust me."

Her mouth thinned. "What do you mean?"

"We've skirted the issue long enough." Maybe too long. He hated the official tone of his voice, hated fucking sounding like an interrogator. "What if Jordan had been here?"

Her chin lifted. "I don't know. I had to trust you. But he wasn't here. You would have been stuck in this cabin together."

"Instead, you and I have been . . . stuck . . . together." He dragged her into his arms and kissed her for a long, satisfying time. Yes, together, he thought, his senses reeling once more from the heady sensation of her embrace.

"Why, Juliana? Why after all this time did you have sex with me?" Damn, what a dumb-ass thing to say. She probably thought he needed to hear how head over heels she was as a sop to his ego. "I mean why did you give in after being so adamant that we're too different, that I remind you of Molly's guys?"

"But you don't remind me of Molly's men. You're the one who said that, not me. You're kind and sexy and honorable and responsible."

"I'm not as wonderful as you think."

"Agreed. You're also a tease and a flirt who'll make a play for anything female."

"You crush me. I haven't been with another woman since I met you. You wiped all other women from my system. You're all I see, all I want."

"And that's why. Do you know what a turn-on it is to be wanted so desperately, so single-mindedly? You overwhelmed me. I didn't want to resist any longer." Her gaze slid away, and her lip trembled, as if she wanted to say more but didn't dare. She slid toward the door. "Um, we have to go. Everything will be all right."

Maybe, maybe not after he said the rest of his speech. He followed her and held the door shut. "Wait, you have to admit the truth about Jordan. I'm helping you find out about him, yes, but it's all pieces of the same puzzle."

"I know that. Wes Vinson and Sudsy Pettit, all tied in with El Águila's operation." She turned aside, her brow pleated. "What do you mean, the truth about Jordan?"

"You can't keep believing your brother is an innocent pawn who can avoid prosecution. For a skeptic, you have on blinders the size of palm fronds." He steeled himself with a deep breath. "The fish truck job lasted a month with two trips a week. All those deliveries weren't to markets and restaurants. He had to know he was a mule, carrying drugs packed with the fish. He may go to prison."

"You're going to arrest him."

"I never made any secret of that. You refuse to believe it. Or to see the truth." He drew in a steadying breath. "You can't separate who I am from my job. From my mission. I'll do what I have to do to get these smugglers. And that includes arresting your brother. I swear to it I'll see he gets a fair shake. Help Jordan by being realistic. My family failed my brother because we failed to be realistic about what he was doing."

They stared at each other for a long moment, the tension as palpable and the atmosphere as cold as the lake.

She retreated a single pace. Her mouth thinned

to a bitter line, and her eyes darkened with emotion he couldn't read. "I was gullible, too trusting. Jordan may have done some illegal things, but that doesn't change what I need to do."

He guessed it was time to reveal what Donovan had dug up. "You feel you have to protect Jordan because you're afraid what happened to your father could happen to him."

Pain filled her gaze. "How long have you known about that?"

"Only since last night's phone call. I know the bare facts. Will you tell me?"

She paced in a circle, hugging herself. Finally she faced him. "When I was in high school, a girl—no one I knew—accused my father of kidnapping her, keeping her prisoner, and raping her. Dad was innocent. While we waited to bail him out of the county jail, the girl's brothers paid guys inside to beat him up." Her voice hitched, and she swallowed hard.

Rick's gut twisted, and he clenched his fists. Shit, he should've dug into her father's history sooner. "God, I'm so sorry."

"The deputies stopped the beating before they killed Dad, but on the way to the hospital, he had a massive heart attack and died." When she looked up, her chin quivered before she firmed it. "Afterward, Dad's accuser said she'd made a mistake and identified another man. Those deputies should've protected Dad. I don't know if Jordan is innocent or guilty, but either way, I fear for his life."

Dios mio. No wonder she wouldn't trust him—or the DEA—to protect her brother. He scraped fingers through his hair. "Juliana, I'll understand if you still won't trust me. What happened to your father was inexcusable. But believe me, your brother is in danger from El Águila's men if they fear he has something on them. If I take Jordan in, he'll be in protective custody because of that danger. I promise to do everything I can to make sure he's safe."

She stared at him for a long minute. "I want to trust you."

His usual smoothness failed him, and his throat constricted. He couldn't get his tongue around the three words he'd never said to any woman. He smoothed a hand over her hair and conjured up a smile. "Thanks for that much."

He had to back off. She was being unreasonable about Jordan, and his explanations didn't punch through her fears. She needed time to see things play out.

Their real differences went to the core of who they were. Her loyalty to her brother and her grief for her father blinded her. For the duration, he couldn't trust her. For damn sure she wouldn't trust him. Hell, she was probably still hiding something from him. Juliana might never trust him. The realization slammed him in the solar plexus.

She said nothing, only watched him with solemn eyes, as if she could read his thoughts. Maybe she could.

He snatched his leather jacket from the wall peg and opened the door.

- 12 -

On Tuesday morning, back at Vinson Seafood, Juliana held the telephone away from her ear and frowned as though the voice on the other end emanated from Mars. After a moment, she placed the receiver in its cradle.

She hadn't slept much so maybe she dreamed the conversation. If only she'd dreamed the rift between her and Rick. They'd driven to Portland in silence thicker than a Maine fog occasionally punctuated by brief, stinging exchanges.

"I didn't lead you on, Juliana," Rick said. "I never pretended I wouldn't arrest Jordan. This thing between us has nothing to do with that."

"It doesn't matter. The attraction was mutual." Chin up, she feigned nonchalance. "You don't need to worry. I'll search Vinson's and cooperate with you—for Jordan's sake. And I don't expect any commitments from you. Or need any."

"Jeez," she whispered. How could she have been so stubborn, so stupid? Yesterday was April first, and she was the Fool. But because of this phone call, maybe she could at least put whatever was between her and Rick on life support.

Miracles didn't fall in her lap every day. Because of a wild coincidence and a trick of fate, she knew where Jordan had stashed himself. He was safe. For the time being.

She offered up silent prayers—one of thanks and one for guidance. She wanted to knock some sense into her brother, knock some responsibility into his thick head. She had to stop propping him up. And she would—once he was home and out of danger.

She'd lain awake last night thinking. Rick was right about Jordan's involvement with the drug dealers. He had to have known what Sudsy Pettit was delivering along with fish. Once she had what the DEA needed from the Vinson files, she'd deliver the evidence and Jordan's hiding place to Rick.

"I can't tell you how glad I am that you're feeling better, Juliana." Wes Vinson grinned as he edged a hip onto the corner of the office manager desk. "For your sake, of course, but you know how much I needed you these past few days."

She hadn't worn blusher to make herself look wan. She crossed mental fingers that he wouldn't detect any deterioration in her amiability toward him. She tapped the computer keyboard, and the printer spewed out documents. "I understand, Wes. These bills will go out today. No problem."

He was hitting on her. She recognized his moves. He perched on her desk for no apparent reason. He offered her his lopsided grin while he talked about nothing.

The fine hairs on her nape rose, and she clasped

her trembling hands together. Was this man going after her because of Jordan? At that noxious idea, poison claws jabbed at her.

She masked her distaste with a tired smile.

Vinson looked up brightly. He might as well have had a cartoon light bulb over his head. *Here it comes.*

"A new restaurant opened up on Exchange Street, Greek food. Hear it's great. Moussaka and stuffed grape leaves and salad with those big black olives. Oh, and baklava. How about staying over tonight and trying it with me?" His enthusiasm had the freckles dancing on his cheeks.

His invitation sounded hopeful for more than dinner. Her skin crawled.

She tilted her head and slumped in regret. Beneath the desk, she curled her fingers so tightly her nails bit into her palms. "Oh, Wes, how nice of you. Thanks, but I can't. I missed classes last week—" she hadn't attended class in much longer than that "—and I have too much to catch up on. And my stomach's still not a hundred percent."

The man shrugged off the rejection with a rain-check offer. After a few moments, he returned to his office.

Behind her, she heard muffled tones, him talking on the phone. She stuffed the bills into their envelopes.

Where might Vinson keep secret, illegal records? In spare moments, she was examining the accounting files. She might decipher some deceptive bookkeeping that Rick couldn't. But she didn't have much time. The *Sea Worthy* would dock in four days.

Although the office manager and two other

employees were still out sick, two clerks flitted around the office like worker bees from computer to file cabinets to the reception desk. Boat captains phoned reporting catches or trooped in with sales receipts and fishy odors from the Portland Fish Exchange.

Marina workers muffled in quilted coveralls and wreathed in the tang of varnish and fiberglass stomped in periodically with demands for orders that hadn't arrived, for resin or paint or electronic equipment Juliana could barely spell on an invoice. Though warm weather remained on the horizon, preparations for the pleasure boating season steamed full speed ahead for Vinson's yacht customers.

Wes had complained about high costs and low profits. If he was involved, he'd hide the contraband-smuggling files somewhere off limits to employees. She knew of only one place. His private office.

She swiveled her desk chair to peek through his open office door. No longer on the phone, he bent over a file drawer behind his desk. A cabinet door normally hid the drawer from sight. The shelf below held not another file drawer but a safe. *A safe.*

Her heart pounded, and her mind spun. Finally. Not that Juliana Paris, master spy, could crack a safe. But maybe she could find the safe combination.

"Hey, it's the Prodigal Son," Jake Wescott called as Rick entered the Boston task force office. "Missed your sorry ass, Cruz."

"Thanks. I missed your ugly mug too." Rick shook the other man's proffered hand. "Glad to be back."

"Been too quiet without you here," Holt Donovan said.

"Wish I could say it's been quiet undercover." Rick shook hands with Donovan and the other agents who filed over.

The chatter of welcome died as agents grabbed coats and headed out. When the room cleared, only Rick, Wescott, and Donovan remained.

Donovan leaned back and propped his boot-clad feet on his desk. "I thought the damned leak was in the GS's brain. But you kept us looking."

Tapping a pencil on his coffee cup, Wescott sat on the edge of Rick's desk. "We grabbed up the leak yesterday. Laurel in Intel."

Laurel was always the one Rick asked to speed up background checks or to trace licenses. "Too bad. Such a quiet little mouse. I liked her." He shook his head ruefully.

Donovan punched his shoulder. "You like all females."

"Even a cornered mouse will bare its teeth," Wescott said.

Donovan frowned. "She had a hot affair with our buddy Carlos Olívas. Met him in a bar. He videotaped them together then blackmailed her. She funneled secure info to him for several months. Given her IT skills, easy enough for her to cover up the whole thing."

And without Juliana's insight, Rick might not have suggested his team look beyond other DEA agents. He'd go tell her that tonight. If she was still speaking to him.

Juliana pulled into her assigned slot in front of her apartment building. As soon as she spotted the cherry red Corvette, her pulse revved.

Rick unfolded himself from the low-slung sports car and sketched a salute. Sliding down the zipper on his black leather jacket, he sauntered over to meet her. A swagger jazzed his gait.

Just seeing him filled some of the hollow places in her heart. It was all she could do not to launch herself into his arms. "Looking good, Agent Cruz. So what's new?"

He wore his official face, but at her query, a spark kindled in his mocha eyes, and his dimple winked with a grin. "Wescott and Donovan found the leak. A clerk in Intel. Blackmailed by Carlos Olívas. That's all I can tell you."

"Oh, Rick, I'm so glad it's over." Her hand involuntarily reached out to him, and she yanked it back before she yielded to her impulse to leap into his arms. No. She'd erected a wall between them and had to keep it propped up. "I didn't see an official car behind me today. Are they no longer protecting me?"

One black brow winged upward. "For some mysterious reason, Olívas seems to have pulled in his horns. No sign of any of those slimeballs for several days now."

"That's a relief. I think." What did it mean? "What do we do now?"

"I owe you big time. How about dinner? We never had a real date." He gave her earring a casual flick.

When it rains, as they say. Two offers for dinner dates in one day. She'd wisely turned down the first, and she shouldn't accept this one.

Rick was mustering all his charm on her behalf. The pirate grin. The bedroom eyes. The tumbled comma of sable hair. Give him a day and he bounced back with more assurance than Wile E. Coyote.

So did that make her the Roadrunner? She was running, all right, from him, from her tangled emotions. From herself.

She didn't have the emotional energy to evade his invitation. Jordan was safe. For now. She'd conceal his secret until she had evidence against Wes Vinson. She did have other information for Rick, so . . .

"I'd love to go out to dinner with you," she heard herself saying. Bad move, but she couldn't resist being with him anymore than she could stop breathing. *I'm my mother's daughter after all.*

He grinned and placed his hand on the small of her back as they entered the building.

His heat penetrated her parka to warm her and tighten her nipples. Once inside her apartment, she flung their coats over a chair back. Being alone with him in the confines of her small apartment too closely resembled being alone in the lake cabin. The sooner they drove to a restaurant—a public place— the better.

Speedy strolled from the bedroom to greet them. With a purr as loud as a blender, he wound his body through Rick's legs.

"He likes me." Rick picked up the animal and

sleeked a hand from head to tail. The cat rumbled even louder.

The sight of his long-fingered hand caressing the brown fur sent tingles down Juliana's back. Retreating to the kitchenette, she poured two glasses of a California merlot Venice had brought over— just in case. Juliana pushed his goblet toward him across the breakfast bar. Keeping that barrier between them might shore up her defenses.

"A quick drink and then we can leave." He deposited Speedy on the floor.

Her pulse beat overtime at his nearness. "You're still grinning. What else happened?"

"The GS—Group Supervisor—usually nails me for not following protocol. But MacMillan was so happy about finding the leak, he agreed to put me in for promotion. Said I was a natural leader."

"Just what your already inflated ego needs." She grinned and clicked glasses with him. "Congratulations."

She lifted her glass to her mouth. A tiny sip was all her fluttery stomach could handle. Lord, she might as well have the words *I know where Jordan is* tattooed across her forehead.

"You have news for me." Rick leaned forward, his elbows on the counter. "You found something today."

As if sensing the mood change, Speedy strolled off with a yowl. Rebuke or accusation at her duplicity.

Juliana jumped at his direct words. Feeling guilty had her forgetting her other news. "Why do you say that?"

"That peaches-and-cream complexion broadcasts

every change of emotion. "What happened? What did you discover?" Rick slipped around the bar and entered the kitchenette. He stood so close to her his breath ruffled her hair. Protective arms drew her against him.

She described how she'd spotted the cabinet safe and file drawer. "I won't have a chance to search there." She shrugged, fighting the need to haul him closer for a kiss.

"He's watching you?"

She cleared her tight throat. "I don't think so. He locks his office when he leaves. I should've seen that clue before."

"Then all we can do is wait until the *Sea Worthy* arrives at the Fish Exchange. In the meantime, you finish out your week at Vinson as an exemplary employee."

"Aye, aye, sir." *Wait? But how can I, when Jordan's life is at stake?*

"Believe me, everything will come out all right. I know you can't bring yourself to trust me. I understand."

She swallowed down bile, tempted to hang her head and tell him he *shouldn't* understand. *How did I dig myself such a hole?* She could tell him about Jordan now, but her instincts said to wait. Yeah, right.

His gaze heated, and tiny gold flames flickered in his eyes. "I've missed you." He lowered his head to kiss her.

"This is a bad idea." She pushed against him, but with no fervor in her protest.

He fitted his lips to hers with the ease of familiarity. She sank into the sensations of his taste, his scent, his magic. He touched his tongue to the corners of her mouth, to the seam as if reacquainting himself with her taste and texture, requesting, not demanding, entry.

And then her tongue was seeking his, and her lips were stroking his as she tried to absorb him. His hand slid beneath her sweater to fit over her lace-covered breast. Heat and need suffused her body.

"Juliana." He clasped her more tightly against him, lifting her off her feet. His arousal nudged her belly.

Shock waves flashed through her nerves, and her senses reeled. Currents of desire arced between them, splintering her walls of defense. Her skin tingled, and she felt suspended on a wave of sensation.

"You can tell me no," he said, his voice a sexy rumble.

Caution is overrated. "You know where the bedroom is."

Swept up, she scarcely knew that he carried her to her bed. Their clothes disappeared as if by magic. Excitement streaked through her at the sensation of his hot skin against her. He lay on top of her, his lean, hard body pressing her into the mattress. Heaven.

She stroked the muscled contours of his back, his firm buttocks as he slowly caressed her breasts. His fingers flowed over her skin, flirted between her legs, enthralled her.

"Juliana, I need you." A moan confirmed his urgency, and she shuddered with delight.

"Rick. *Yes.*" When he slid into her, she was more than ready.

Her body, her soul burned. Their bodies moved

in sync, striving, stroking with the same urgency. She savored his possession, his devouring of her, wished it could last. Tension coiled inside her and sensation spread out from her center and rolled through her in a huge wave. He tensed, gave a hoarse shout, and joined her in release.

On a satisfied sigh, he sank down, pressing his forehead to hers. "That was beyond powerful. You take me places I never knew existed. My Juliana." He collapsed to one side. He tucked his head beside hers, close enough to nuzzle her ear.

She was beyond examining his enigmatic statement, beyond examining her reasons for succumbing. She would just enjoy him and this time together.

He smiled. "It's not too late to go out. I think I've worked up an appetite."

She kissed him, her limbs heavy, her heart filled. She was satisfied to the core of her being, but his touch rekindled desire.

At an insistent chirping, Rick ended their embrace. "Damn." He set her gently away from him, then reached to the floor for his pants.

"Cruz," he snapped into his phone.

Barely aware of his conversation, she struggled to recover her senses. She lay boneless on the bed.

What a weak-willed ninny I am. On her competing lists, she had at least ten reasons for not falling in love with him, for not even kissing him. On the other side, only one. She couldn't even put into words why she found it hard to deny him, to deny her feelings?

"That was Jake Wescott." Rick tucked away the phone. The frown etched into his brow transformed his face into his cop expression. "Cops found a man who'd been beaten. He's at Maine Medical Center. Has a driver's license belonging to Finnegan Farnham."

Her heart plummeted into her stomach. *"Finny?"*

- 13 -

Rick demanded speed from all 345 horses in his 'Vette's 5.7 liter V-8, but the trip from Portsmouth to Portland seemed like four hours instead of less than one. *Por Dios*, spring arrived slowly here. The beginning of April and the trees still had no buds. Dirty clumps of snow on the roadsides added to the dreary pall of the gray skies.

A glance at Juliana, huddled in the passenger seat, didn't reassure him. Something other than what she'd told him was bothering her. She'd said no more than two words about why Jordan's buddy had popped up in Portland when he was supposed to be aboard a trawler somewhere between Cape Cod and the Canadian border. Did she know the reason? Or only suspect, as he did?

He found a parking space in the visitor lot, across the street from MMC, a sprawling brick complex in Portland's West End.

As they pushed through the glass doors, Rick's past slammed into him. The squeak of rubber soles down the black and white tiled corridors. Odors of institutional bland food, lemon cleanser, and sickness. Hushed voices comforted relatives or discussed clinical findings. Chatty voices planned a day off.

All of that brought back memories. "I've avoided hospitals since my *papá* paraded me through South Shore Hospital to show off his son the future doctor."

She gave him a wry smile. "He pushed. And you rebelled."

"I was just a stand-in for Rudy. He would have been the doctor. If he'd lived." Back then his father's rigidity had made him angry. Today the familiar odors and sounds triggered no pain, only mild resentment.

She squeezed his hand. "You had to do what was right for you. He must have feared he'd lose another son to violence."

Rick's heart stopped. Juliana perceived a possibility that had never occurred to him. Fear could've been the reason for his father's censure, for his seeming lack of caring. "That was years ago. Returning to Miami, and his disapproval, no longer has the power over me it once did."

"Where's the room?"

Her agitated voice and peach scent dispersed the memories, and he picked up their pace. An elevator and a maze of corridors led them to the room labeled F. Farnham. Medical personnel in pastel tunics whisked past them with medicine carts and IV stands. A uniformed cop slouched in a chair beside the door.

Before Rick could address him, a Portland-based

DEA agent walked toward them from a lounge at the end of the hall. Someone's fist had once rearranged the burly agent's nose into a bulbous mass. "Yo, Cruz, I had word you'd be coming. Glad you got everything straightened out in your office." He thrust out a hand.

Rick gripped his hand. "Thanks, Harriman. How's it going?"

"The man in there, how badly is he hurt?" Juliana unzipped her parka, then shifted her backpack to one shoulder. Her haunted gaze made Rick want to pull her close.

Agent Harriman gave a low whistle. "When his beak heals, it's gonna look worse than mine. No serious internal damage though. Whoever did this worked him over pretty good, but they wanted him conscious. Doc says if Farnham's broken ribs don't affect his lungs, he'll be all right. Besides that, concussion, couple broken fingers, cigarette burns on his chest."

Juliana gave a horrified gasp.

Rick yielded to instinct and looped an arm around her shoulders. She pressed closer, elevating his mood a notch. *She* might not trust him, but her body did.

"Kid's got guts," the agent continued. "Hid in his rooms for two, three days trying to deal with his injuries alone. When the landlady came to collect the rent, she called an ambulance and the cops."

"Wonder if he spilled what they wanted to hear." Rick turned toward the patient's door. "He conscious?"

"They're keeping him doped up. For the pain. Don't know what you can get out of him. But see for yourselves." Harriman shifted his feet and rolled his shoulders.

Rick pushed the door inward for Juliana to precede him.

MMC had made an effort to create a soothing environment. But this patient couldn't appreciate the watercolors of coastal scenes adorning the yellow walls. Swathed in bandages, he lay flat on his back, his multihued, puffy eyelids closed. An IV stand dripped meds into a vein in his left arm, which lay limply on the green blanket covering him. That hand was encased in bandages.

"Oh, the poor kid." Juliana pressed fingers to her mouth. Tears flowed.

Finny. This kid was stocky, not gangly like Jordan Paris. Finny being here confirmed Rick's hunch of Jordan's location. Apprehension and a sinking foreboding mingled in his gut.

"Wh-who's that?" a voice croaked from the bed. Farnham's eyes opened, slits in a devastated landscape.

Stepping closer, Rick explained their presence. The tang of burn medication and alcohol swabs feathered the air. "If you're Finnegan Farnham, I have to ask you some questions."

"I'm Finny . . . Shoulda stayed up north." His gaze shifted to Juliana. "You're Jules." He reached toward her with his good right hand.

"Jordan calls me that sometimes." Juliana clasped his hand. "What happened to you?"

"Them Mexicans . . . waited for me at my place." He drew a rattling breath, started again. "Jordan warned me . . . My dumb-ass mistake. I'm sorry. Didn't want to. I told . . ." His voice was fading.

"*What* did you tell them? Where's Jordan?" Rick wished he could shake it out of him. He knew the answer, but he needed to hear it.

Finny's head lolled against the pillow. His eyes closed. He was slipping into Demerol-induced sleep.

The crucial bit of information, and they were losing him, dammit. "*Farnham*, hang on, man. Tell us where Jordan is," he urged. "He's in danger. Help us find him."

Juliana squeezed Finny's hand in a silent plea. But he was asleep. She released his hand and stepped away. "I can tell you where Jordan is." Her whisper was barely audible.

"What did you say?" He was afraid to hear the answer.

She turned away from him, her muscles bowstring tight, shoulders rigid. "They traded places. He's on the *Sea Worthy*."

He'd begun to suspect exactly that, but her words rocked him like a ship's wake. Fuckin'-A. Jordan had been on board the dragger all this time, safe from the gang and invisible to authorities. No wonder the fish buyer didn't recognize Finny's photograph. He'd never been there.

Rick would laugh if the implications weren't so dire. Once Olívas found Finny, he had no need to shadow Juliana. All he had to do was wait for the dragger to arrive in Portland. Same thing the DEA was waiting for.

"Let's go." Gripping her arm, he ushered her from the room just as a scrubs-clad nurse entered. His mouth taut, he marched Juliana into the lounge.

"You *knew*."

"I—"

"You knew it was Jordan on the fishing boat. That's why you were so certain he couldn't be the one in the hospital bed. You knew where he was." He stabbed a finger at her in accusation.

"You don't understand." Wringing the strap of her backpack, she stood in the center of the sparsely furnished lounge. She looked distraught and defenseless—and guilty.

"No, I think I finally do understand. I suspected. Did you know where Farnham was and when he'd return? If we'd known that, we could have headed him off. You could have saved that poor kid in there."

"You're wrong." Her chin rose in defiance. "I found out about their switch only today. Too late for Finny."

"Today." The tension vising his head eased a notch. How?"

"The Rockland fish buyer, the one we talked to, called the office. A problem with his invoice. Something prompted me to ask him again about Finny. He insisted there was no Finny on the boat. When I asked him to describe the crew, he said he hardly remembered them except for one with two different colored eyes."

"What does that mean?" He paced a circle around her. *What the hell else don't I know?*

"Jordan has one brown eye and one green. He sometimes wears a colored contact because people look at him weird. Even his driver's license has green for eye color. The man the buyer described had to be him."

"Why didn't I know about this eye color thing before?"

"It never came up. I didn't think it was important."

"You mean you didn't want me to know. Still hoping to get to him first?"

"I don't know. Everything was so complicated, so scary. I thought I had time to—"

"Make a few lists? Add a balance sheet?" He stopped pacing and glared at her. She didn't trust him, but after their intimacy, this betrayal cut deep.

Juliana turned her back and hugged herself. "I'm sorry. It's not you. When you said Finny'd been beaten, I wasn't certain who I'd see in that hospital bed. I'd have told you—soon."

"*Soon.*" He scraped fingers through his hair. "Not good enough." A lump of pain congealed in his gut. He'd been right in the first place. He never should have allowed his hormones to confuse his judgment about a woman with family ties to the drug trade.

"I know, but it's all I have." She faced him again. "What will you do now? Send the Coast Guard out to arrest him?"

He barked a bitter laugh. "Why should I tell you anything? You don't trust me. And obviously *I* can't trust *you.*"

Juliana turned the spare key she'd kept and slipped inside Vinson Enterprises. As she'd expected for a Saturday, the offices remained dark and empty. He must be somewhere setting up an alibi, in case Olívas implicated him when the DEA pounced. Maybe he didn't suspect the DEA was on to him.

The wall clock's hands were straight up. Noon.

Sea Worthy was due in. Rick and other DEA agents could be surrounding El Águila's gang. And putting the cuffs on Jordan. Her pulse jittered, but she breathed deeply for calm. *I can do nothing about that.*

Rick.

At the thought, his image floated before her. The way she wanted to remember him, no bitter look of disappointment on his face. He wasn't the worthless charmer she'd imagined. He was honorable and dedicated and she'd lost any chance with him. He'd begun to trust her and she'd ruined it. Ruined everything.

A pain sharp as a needle pierced her heart. She pressed a clammy palm to her mouth and banished thoughts of him. She'd messed things up and this was her only chance to make repairs, however slight, however late.

Leaving the lights off, she tiptoed through the office to her desk. She booted up the computer. Vinson might have the safe combination stored somewhere in the files. Then she could get in—as long as he hadn't changed the password.

A few minutes later, she found a file listing only a series of numbers. Maybe.

Her nerves were jumping like spring peepers at dusk. *Safe cracking. Not the best strategy for a future accountant, but here goes.* She left the computer running in case she had to search again. Knees wobbling, she crept to the boss's office door.

She tried not to think of worst-case scenarios but her brain wouldn't stop conjuring them. Vinson could show up. The *Sea Worthy*'s captain could pop in with his receipts. The key she'd snitched from the key cabinet might not work. Maybe it wasn't for this office at all. Her heart drummed so hard she clutched her chest.

Get going. Get it over with.

She fumbled the key, but finally the lock clicked. The office door opened. She shut her eyes briefly.

With the blinds closed, a twilight-like gloom blanketed Vinson's office. The big wooden desk with its phalanx of greenery, the conference table, chairs, and cabinets looked normal. The musty smell of potting soil and the oiliness of stale coffee permeated the space.

She hurried across the carpeted floor to the cabinet behind the desk.

On her knees, she opened the door concealing the safe. Too dark to see the dial. Dammit, she should have brought a flashlight. She'd never replaced the one Rick broke when he jumped her at her brother's apartment.

She slid the desk lamp over to the near corner. A punch of the button in its base, and a spotlight glared on her guilty face. And on the safe. Surely not enough light to be seen outside.

Before touching the dial, she listened to the office. The computer's hum, the furnace's low rumble, a cricket's chirp. Nothing else. Her fingers closed on the cold steel.

Firming her resolve, she spun the dial and twisted to the first number. The second. The third. Her ears and fingers weren't sensitive enough to know if the combination worked. Hand trembling, she reached for the handle and pulled down.

The handle clicked. The steel safe door swung toward her.

A shadowy movement behind her brought her

head around.

The world crashed down on the side of her head.

White-hot pain exploded. Colors bloomed behind her eyelids, then stygian black.

- 14 -

Rick shivered in the raw morning as he watched the *Sea Worthy* chug toward the fish pier. He zipped his raid jacket up to the neck. Weather forecasters predicted clearing skies for Saturday, but in true Maine style, the April weather remained overcast in a slate gray that matched the Casco Bay waters.

Constant activity around the several piers made it easy for the DEA to plant agents dressed as fishermen and dock workers in strategic spots. Neither Jordan nor Olívas's men would escape capture this time.

As soon as the *Sea Worthy*'s crew tied up, agents swarmed aboard. Jake Wescott escorted the captain from the dragger. "No sign of Jordan Paris. Or his gear."

"Not on board?" Rick roared at the captain.

"Got off last port." A weathered man of indeterminate age, he took a long drag on a cigarette.

It was all Rick could do not to beg a butt from

him. Instead, he surreptitiously inhaled the smoke in hopes of easing his hyper nerves.

"You were harboring a suspected criminal. Unless you want your boat searched from stem to stern and turned inside out, you'd better tell me where Paris went." Rick paused for effect. "We might have to search anyway if we find any hint you're hauling anything but fish."

The captain's seamed face crumpled. He tossed down his smoke and stomped on it. "I don't know what you think this guy did, this Paris or Finny or whatever his name is. My boat's clean. I got nothin' to hide. We docked in Portsmouth yesterday to take on fuel. A message was waitin' for him. Said he had to leave, some emergency at home. That's all I know."

Questioning wrung no more from the captain or crew. No one saw Jordan Paris leave the docks or knew who might've picked him up—Juliana or the Mexicans. *She wouldn't, not after* . . . Too painful to contemplate.

"More bad news." Agent Harriman's dour countenance greeted him.

"Don't tell me." The knot in Rick's gut warned him about Jordan's fate. "No Olívas."

"Right in one." The Portland agent waved a beefy arm toward the Exchange's fenced parking area and the street beyond. "We'll hang out awhile longer in case they're late."

Rick doubted the necessity. Somehow the Mexicans had finessed Jordan right into their trap. The only silver lining was the connection to Wes Vinson. How else could they have known where to find the *Sea Worthy*? A narrow silver lining glimmered in his mind. If the Mexicans had Jordan, it meant Julian wasn't complicit.

But how could he face her with the news? He dug his knuckles into his temples to fight off the headache that threatened. His phone buzzed inside his jacket. The Boston office.

"I have a strange message for you," the receptionist said. "From a Venice Aaron."

His heart skipped a beat. "Shoot."

"She says Juliana Paris could be in danger. The caller said Ms. Paris rushed out this morning saying something about wanting to help, to make up for not telling you about Jordan. Something about evidence. The Aaron woman says her friend doesn't answer her phone. Calls go to voice mail. Does this make sense to you?"

"Unfortunately, yes." He thanked her and disconnected. Acid burned in his veins. He hissed in a breath.

Juliana might have found more evidence than she could handle.

Awareness chewed into Juliana's brain with burning bites. Her eyelids fluttered open to a swarm of black spots. When she tried to sit up, her arms wouldn't work. Her stomach lurched, and her heart thumped wildly.

"Take it easy, Jules. You all right?"

Oh, God, Jordan. Yes!

Unable to speak, she flopped back down like a landed cod. Deep breaths fought back nauseating dizziness. Throbbing pain radiated from her neck and shoulder and bounced around in her head like a spiked ball.

A louvered vent admitted scant light. She lay on a cement floor in a windowless metal room the size of a walk-in closet. A shed maybe. Metal and cement refrigerated this space to nearly freezing. In a corner was a stack of boxes and her backpack.

Her hands were bound behind her, the reason for the numbness. And her feet were tied. Not a landed cod. More of a trussed turkey. She was cold and sore. And aware that the two of them had landed in deep shit.

"You okay?" Jordan crawled and rolled closer, his face contorted with the effort.

Her joy at seeing Jordan alive battled with her distress at their predicament.

Someone, probably Wes Vinson, the crooked bum, had hit her over the head as she opened the safe. She was so intent on the combination she missed hearing him enter the office. Her last-second flinch at his movement spared her a concussion. Instead of her skull, his knockout blow had connected mostly with her neck.

"I've been better," she said. "How did you get here?"

With a grimace, Jordan pushed back to prop himself against the wall. His lip was cut, and he looked as gray as the cement, but in better shape than Finny. Grease and blood stained his hooded sweatshirt and jeans. His boots were scraped and scarred. His legs weren't hobbled like hers, but moving around made his pain worse. What had they done to him?

"I'm sorry you got caught up in this, Jules. Last thing I expected. I guess it means you know about

Sudsy and the drug hauls."

She started to nod, but swirling pain changed her mind. "I also know about Vinson and the Mexicans. Now tell me how they captured you."

"I got a note from Finny that I should leave the boat in Portsmouth. They'd be waiting for me in Portland. It was a fake. They grabbed me on the dock. We're in a boat shed at Vinson's marina."

She lay still and closed her eyes. "Drugs. Dammit, Jordan. How did it happen? Why?"

He shook his head, his grimy blond hair hanging in wormy strands around his dirt-smeared face. "I needed the work, so I wouldn't have to keep sponging off you. It seemed like a straight gig at first. But then things got dicey and I couldn't quit."

He related a tale of deliveries to markets, restaurants, and back alleys, of his gradual tumbling to the real nature of the deliveries. When he tried to quit, Sudsy Pettit threatened him. Finally he got up the nerve to tell the man to shove it.

He happened on a meeting at the diner beside Vinson's—Sudsy, Wes Vinson, and a Mexican who might have been Carlos Olívas. "They saw me, Jules. I had to run. That's when I phoned you."

"Not because you had any evidence against them, just because you saw them together." Was that all he had on them?

"That Mexican guy chased me. I yelled to him that I had a cell-phone picture of the three of them together. Said I'd give it to the cops. He slowed down at that. Enough for me to get away in the crowd on Commercial Street."

A snapshot. For that they'd searched his apartment and hers.

"You always were fast on your feet." With bittersweet warmth, she recalled the times he used to race with her when he was in high school.

"Runs in the family."

When she frowned at their banter, a vise tightened at the base of her skull. "Unless we get out of this, we may never run again. We have to do something."

"Shh, he's coming." Face pinched with pain and fear, he turned toward the steel door.

A key clanked on a padlock, and then the door swung open.

Dapper in his crisp jeans and topsiders, Vinson entered. A small silver pistol rode at his belt. "Awake, are we?"

"No thanks to you." She made an attempt at a snarl, but her pain-contorted expression probably looked more like a cramp.

"Too bad you got so nosy, Juliana. We could have had a good time together."

"Don't give me that," she spat. "You hired me, hit on me to find out about Jordan."

He knelt to check her wrists. "I should've known better."

The thought of them together repelled her to the point of nausea. She wanted to spit in his face, but that would that get her zip. Rather than attack him from her vulnerable position, she had to try to reach him. "Why, Wes? Did you get hooked yourself? You can get help."

"Me? Drugs?" He sneered at the idea. "I'm not dumb." He stared almost wistfully out the door toward the bay. "The short answer is money."

Inspiration struck with one of the drumbeats

pounding inside her head. "Let us go before you get in deeper. I e-mailed the DEA office about what I found in the safe."

With an ugly laugh, he sat on his heels. "Nice try, but you'd barely opened the door when I found you."

She schooled her voice. "You have it backwards. I was putting things back, ready to close the safe. The cops and the DEA should be here any minute." As long as he didn't quiz her about the safe contents, it was a good bluff.

Doubt creased his freckled forehead. He still looked boyishly handsome.

He checked Jordan's wrists, then stood and leered down at her. "Bitch. They won't find anything. Most of all they won't find you. Or your stupid brother. The Mexicans will help me load you on board my yacht, and then the three of us will take a little cruise."

Satisfied their bonds were tight, he left them to stew about their fate.

As soon as Rick saw Juliana's car at Debby's Diner, he knew she'd been caught. Vinson's SUV sat in the marina parking lot beside the familiar type of nondescript rental car favored by Olívas. Claws raked his gut, and he spat out a string of Spanish and English curses. He signaled the other flak-vested and raid-jacketed teams.

They fanned out around the Vinson buildings so none of the suspects could escape. A Coast Guard boat waited in the harbor.

Donovan and Wescott went with Rick. The SIG

held in a two-handed grip, he ran to the office entrance. No sign of anyone. The offices remained dark and quiet.

Thumps resounded from the long metal boat building to their left. He gestured at the other two to follow him. Low and quiet, they edged along the building to its open bay door.

Donovan stayed with him, behind a pile of rope. Wescott ducked around a forklift. When ready, he waved to Rick.

Before Rick could move, a man walked from the structure's open bay. Almost as tall as he, but heavier and darker. Rick knew the son of a bitch's face as well as his own—El Águila's number one henchman, Carlos Olívas.

Juliana forced down panic at Vinson's insinuation of a cruise. From which she and Jordan would not return.

They had no time to waste. They had to get free. "What did they tie us with?"

"Sisal rope here, but Vinson used duct tape on you."

She blinked at the silvery band around her ankles. Turning her head gingerly, she gauged whether she could reach her backpack. Beside it sat the roll of tape.

Lying back, she nearly giggled. "He used the duct tape from my own bag."

"Yup. You still carry everything in the world?"

"You're thinking what I'm thinking, Jordan? If I can manage to root around in that bag, we might get out of here yet. Then you can turn that picture over to the cops, the DEA, and whatever other authorities are in on this."

"Um, there *is* no picture. I said that to save my neck."

Figured. She fought back the urge to warn him about his penchant for acting on impulse. If they managed to live, just maybe he'd remember that little lesson.

At the first attempt at scooting, pain ripped through her neck and head, and nausea crept up her throat. Black spots swam again, and she forced herself not to hyperventilate.

Dammit, she wouldn't let the bastards win. She could do this.

Inch by agonizing inch, she slid over to her pack. Vinson had left it open. No catch to deal with. She plunged her hands through the contents—day planner, brush, wallet, calculator, ibuprofen, lipsticks—multi-blade knife.

Clutching the knife, she struggled to sit. At first the room swam before her eyes. *Come on, come on.* Slowly she forced away the queasiness and focused on what she had to do.

"Hurry, Jules. I don't know how long they'll leave us here." His strained voice sounded so young.

She plucked open the special serrated blade. It slipped, but she caught it, slicing the tip of her left index finger. She clamped her lips against the sting. She scraped the blade at the tape's edge. "Jordan, talk to me. Tell me about the *Sea Worthy.* Tell me how you and Finny switched places."

The process was slow. Her fingers and wrists cramped, but she kept going in rhythm with her brother's narrative and the throbbing in her head.

"They needed someone on the *Sea Worthy*. Finny wanted to go ice fishing at his uncle's camp at Moosehead Lake. The captain and crew didn't know either one of us."

Twice more she cut herself. Blood trickled, warm and slick over the tape and her fingers. Her hands were slippery with sweat and blood, and the handle kept oozing from her grip. She gritted her teeth and sawed. "And you needed a place to hide."

"I was safe enough aboard. I like being at sea. But how did you find out about the drugs, Jules?"

Pausing to catch her breath, she closed her eyes in pain. "I've been trying to find you ever since you called. Both the Mexicans and the DEA involved me whether I liked it or not."

"The drug gang? Why the hell did *they* bother *you*?"

"Use your brain, little brother. Even you should be able to add this one up." She hated the bitterness in her voice, but energy was flagging, and her head contained the devil's steel band live in concert.

Dawning comprehension raised his sandy brows. "Oh. To get to me. To get the picture." He slumped lower against the wall.

"No harm done to me, at least up to now." She'd tell him about Finny later. "I have myself to blame for this particular sorry state of affairs. I was snooping where I shouldn't have been. At least we're together." She struggled again with the tiny knife.

No harm done, except to my heart. Not El Águila's men, but Ricardo Cruz had provided the highest drama of her whole life. He didn't want her any more. He didn't trust her. If she lived through this, life without him would be as dark and empty as a black hole.

To distract from the wounds inside her she sawed harder at the gooey tape.

"I don't get why they bugged you. You didn't know where I was." His voice sounded petulant, typical of his self-absorption, his callow perception.

"Jeez, they didn't believe that. The DEA had to protect me for weeks. And what did you plan to do once the boat returned? Didn't you know they'd be waiting for you?"

He lifted one shoulder in a sheepish shrug. "I didn't think about it. Figured I'd be safe aboard. No one knew me as anything but Finny. Dammit, why did he tell them where I was?"

That stopped her. "They put him in the hospital. He's lucky to be alive."

With a groan, he sank lower on the dirty floor. "I really screwed up this time."

She didn't deny it or try to comfort him. The knife severed the last strings of tape. She peeled it away from her wrists and eased her arms stiffly forward to massage her hands and arms. Then she freed her ankles, an easier and less bloody task. She shivered at the cold and damp seeping into her bones. Her headache was slowly ebbing. Enough that she could stand, though her knees had post-marathon wobble.

Jordan slumped while she struggled with his bonds. The coarse rope took longer than the tape, but eventually she freed him.

"We have to figure out how to get out of this shed or warehouse or whatever it is." She hooked an arm under his shoulder. "Let me help you stand.

You have to get off that cement."

Jordan didn't budge, made no effort to rise. "I can't."

"What do you mean? Why not?"

"They broke my leg. When they kidnapped me in Portsmouth, the fuckers didn't have anything to tie me up with, so they slammed the damn van door on me. I can't walk. I can't even stand."

- 15 -

Hands in the air, Olívas." Rick aimed the SIG. "Don't move."

"You got nothing on me, Cruz," the Mexican said in Spanish. But he obeyed, fists clenched, body tensed.

"Speak English, you bastard. We got more than you think." Rick didn't see a weapon, but hesitated to move forward and frisk the guy. Who else was in that metal building? "Now walk toward me— slowly."

El Águila's man walked closer, but kept shifting his glance toward the boat building's open door. When he came within a few feet, he dove headfirst at Rick's midsection.

Rick sidestepped, then aimed a kick. His foot grazed the man's temple.

Olívas grabbed for the gun. Rick hung on and tripped him. The two men fell to the asphalt in a welter of tangled limbs. A small automatic fell from the smuggler's waistband and clanked on the pavement. Rick kicked it away.

Olívas landed a few good blows to Rick's belly and one to his jaw, but Rick held onto his weapon. His middle-aged opponent was strong and tough. A dirty fighter and desperate, but untrained.

Fury fueled Rick's strength, fury at all this gang had done to his brother, to Juliana's brother, to countless others. He delivered a solid chop to the other man's throat, and he collapsed like a tent.

"Well done, Cruz." Donovan's voice came from above him. He handed Rick a pair of zip-tie handcuffs.

"What took you so long? I could have used some fucking help." He pushed the coughing Olívas over onto his face and fastened the plastic bands around his wrists. Then he stripped his captive of an ankle sheath knife.

"We thought you needed to throw a few punches at someone." The cowboy shot a pointed glance toward his left. "Besides, we were a little busy ourselves."

Two more Hispanic men lay prone like their boss.

"Where'd you find them?"

"In the big building there." Wescott nodded toward its entrance. "Wait until you see what else is inside. Looks like we were right about the source of the heroin problem in Maine. Long wooden boxes that probably held some of the stolen M-16s and XM-8s." A beaming smile spread across his countenance as if he'd won the lottery.

"Carlos, you've been a busy boy." Rick yanked his captive to his feet. "Seems we have plenty on you after all."

"You got no fuckin' case." The man sneered. "If you foun' drugs, they belon' to this Vinson, not me. My lawyer will free me before you can do paperwork."

Rick smiled. "You're caught with the goods this time. I wouldn't count on your esteemed *líder* on this one. After this, you may prefer prison to what he arranges for you."

"Rick," Wescott said, "no sign of Juliana. Or Vinson."

"El Águila want me dead? I don' believe you." Dread and doubt lurked in the depths of the man's dark eyes, marking him a decade older than middle age.

"No skin off my nose. Besides, rumor has it El Águila has gone into hiding, with the Federales in pursuit." Rick curled his fist in the slimeball's shirt and tugged, hoping he trapped chest hairs. "Now tell me where the woman is, or we'll stop playing nice."

All pretense of bravado gone, Olívas whined, "I don' know. Vinson said he'd take care of her and her brother. Somethin' about a one-way boat trip."

Juliana helped Jordan slide closer to the door. Hefting her backpack, she wished she had her binoculars. Oh God, the bag had to be heavy enough to do its job.

A moment later, a clunk of the padlock announced their captor's return.

Jordan angled his arms behind him as if still bound.

Pulse roaring in her ears like storm surf, Juliana

waited behind the door.

The door swung inward, and Vinson stalked in, his gun in one hand. In his other he carried an open gasoline can. "No time for a cruise," he announced with a grimace that transformed his features from benign to sinister. "This'll look like some snoops got caught in their own fire."

Juliana stepped around the door's edge. With all her might, she swung the backpack at Vinson's belly.

Jordan grabbed the man's ankles and yanked.

Wes Vinson executed a perfect banana-peel flip. With a whale spout of exhalation, he landed on his back. The pistol blasted a deafening shot into the metal roof.

Gasoline splashed from the dropped can in a small fountain and spread across the floor.

The pungent odor stung Juliana's nostrils and snapped her from the shock of what had just happened. She righted the can, then plucked the pistol from her victim's hand.

Shaking like a flag in a March wind, she held it in two hands as she'd seen Rick do.

"Jules, he's out cold." Jordan peered at Vinson, lying on his back. "He must have cracked his skull on the cement."

"Serves him right for beaning me, but I'm not taking the gun off him yet. We have to get out of here and call for help. Drag yourself away from this gasoline."

She waited while he edged past the other man's still form. Dragging his injured leg, her brother crawled out the door. Sweat beaded his forehead. In spite of his adolescent mistakes, his bravery made tears well in her eyes.

Damn you, Vinson, damn you to hell. How did she ever think of him as pleasant and charming? Lying there, he looked harmless, but he'd been about to kill them both. To burn them alive. Hot tears stung and nausea burned. She slumped, lowering the gun.

Vinson surged up. "Bitch!" He plowed a fist into her shoulder. "You won't stop me."

Pain detonated through her arm. She folded to the gasoline-soaked floor. The gun skittered away with a metallic shriek.

"Juliana!" Jordan yelled, but his voice came from far, far away, as if through padded walls.

Her brain did a slow, sickening spiral. The black spots returned, buzzing in her head and before her eyes.

"A shot." Rick spun toward the report. *Juliana.* If Vinson hurt her, he'd— "Where did it come from?"

"Over there." Wescott started running. "Behind the offices."

Rick issued terse orders into his radio as he sprinted in that direction.

A dozen DEA agents and cops converged on the metal shed behind the Vinson office building. At the tableau ahead, Rick froze, gun cocked. He held up a hand to halt the others.

Outside the shed a sweat-shirt-clad guy dragged himself toward a nine-millimeter Glock. *Jordan Paris.*

Two struggling figures on the ground blocked the doorway. *Vinson and Juliana.*

It should have been a very lopsided fight, but it wasn't. On his back, Vinson levered himself against the door frame in an effort to reach the pistol. Juliana strangled his legs with one arm. She was whacking him in the nuts with her backpack. Against her weight, the son of a bitch couldn't move forward or make it to his feet.

Juliana's tenacity was incredible. Rick dashed forward and scooped up the Glock.

Wescott and Donovan pulled Jordan Paris out of the way.

Snarling in frustration, Vinson heaved back a fist. "Bitch."

Rick blocked his arm, jammed the SIG under his jaw. "Don't even think about it, dirtbag. I don't fucking need an excuse."

Other agents moved in and hauled the marina owner away.

Rick lifted Juliana into his arms and carried her from the volatile fumes.

"My brother, he's in shock. They . . . they broke his leg." A sob burst from her, and tears flooded his collar.

He hugged her closer and called to Wescott to send for an ambulance. "I'll get you both blankets."

"You sh-should put me down. I'm soaked. You'll get gasoline all over you."

She was safe. She was okay, really okay if the little fool was worried about his clothes.

The coppery taste of terror subsided with the slowing of his heartbeat. He sank his nose into her hair, seeking the peach scent beneath the gasoline. "Hush, *mi brava*, and let me hold you."

Agents read Miranda rights to all the scumbags, five

counting Jordan, who was the only one not handcuffed. He'd keep until he was treated, but the Mexicans and Vinson were ready to be processed. Vinson stalked to the DEA van muttering complaints about the unfairness of it all and his inability to make a damned profit when the fishing was so lousy and government regulations stymied him at every turn.

"Ninety percent of these assholes find a way for their crimes to be someone else's fault," Rick said.

"And the world fucking owes them a living," Jake Wescott agreed.

"Not just a living, a profit, to hear that bastard spout off," Holt Donovan added.

Rick had little time to see to Juliana other than wrapping a blanket around her. He had evidence to bag and label and other agents to direct. On autopilot, he did his job, but kept one anxious eye on the small wool-wrapped figure hovering near her brother.

The EMTs declared she probably needed stitches. In spite of Rick's urging, she refused treatment. "I need to go home and have a bath. I'll be all right."

He telephoned later, but Venice said she'd patched up Juliana and she was sleeping.

The next day when he made it back to the Boston Division office, he discovered his transfer had arrived.

"Great, just great." He slumped at his desk. Everything was coming together—Portland case solved, Olívas and his gang off the streets, his transfer.

Everything but Juliana.

NEVER SURRENDER

- 16 -

Juliana emerged from the wooded slopes of the Otter Mountain West Face Trail.

The view always soothed and thrilled her. This April afternoon was no exception. Fir and pine-spiked hills undulated like a rumpled blanket down, down to the choppy Atlantic. Over the Cranberry Isles, cerulean skies arched to the indigo horizon. Lobster boats churned to their bright buoy-marked traps.

She'd hiked up slowly, drinking in the forest's calm, its sweet scent of new growth, and enjoying the small signs of spring—leaf buds on the birches and tiny green leaves on the forest floor, dogtooth violets and bunchberry. Before knowing Rick, she'd never taken the time to enjoy their beauty.

Today she was noticing it alone.

Three days after the drug gang's capture and Jordan's arrest, matters calmed enough for her to escape for a few days. Jordan was out of the hospital and out on bail, charged with drug trafficking. She'd heard the task force still had nothing on the weapons. But for the drugs, Jordan could tell them where all the drops were, who all the buyers were. He'd identified the other body, another young mule duped by Sudsy Pettit.

Her brother was home, in her apartment, being pampered by Molly, who had arrived and suddenly developed maternal instincts. Timely, if ironic. Clucking about infection, Molly dragged her to the hospital for stitches on her hand. Now her wounds were healing. She had to get away, to come here to sort out her feelings and her future.

And begin to heal her heart.

Easing off her pack, she sat on a sun-drenched rock. She slipped off her windbreaker and tied it at her waist. Her heart ached for all she'd found and lost. She pressed her palms to the butterfly decal on her tee-shirt.

Rick had called her his *mariposa*, his butterfly, and in his arms she had flown high, she had dared, she had broken out of her staid little mold to see with new perspective. The security and stability she longed for were in the love and trust between a man and woman. Like a wooden boat against this rocky coast, her dissembling had shattered hope of that for her and Rick.

She wanted to sit here where she'd climbed with Rick. Today she wanted to remember. Memories were all she had. She opened herself to the mountain's peace.

Rick barreled from the tree cover. When he spotted her seated on *their* boulder, his heart stuttered an extra beat. He stumbled to a stop. His gaze zeroed in on her. On her soft pink mouth, open in shock at the clattering he'd made on the trail.

Gut churning, he mustered his best piano-key smile. "*Hola*, Juliana." He flopped down beside her.

"What are you doing here?" Her teeth fretted her lower lip as she glared at him.

He caressed her skin, especially that extra soft spot beneath the curve of her jaw. "Your uncle said I could find you here."

Distrust and apprehension rode on her forehead, but he felt a kernel of hope in her shiver at his touch. He leaned back and turned his face to the sun. "What a day!"

She glanced back at the trail. "You *ran* up the mountain."

Nodding, he clasped her fluttering hands. "Because *you* are here."

"Rick, I—"

"Hush." He leaned closer to brush a kiss over her lips. "Let me do this right. Another reason I came today was to apologize. I was wrong to push you so hard about your brother. The blinders that focused me on avenging my brother's death kept me from considering your need to protect your brother. Forgive me for not understanding."

She shook her head. "There's nothing to forgive. I should have trusted you."

"I shouldn't have expected you to trust me. And I didn't, couldn't trust you."

Her mouth turned up in a shaky half smile. "So it's a stalemate."

"Not quite. I know you're worthy of trust. I hope you can trust me enough to build from there over the next fifty years or so. Together." He lifted her fingers to his lips.

"This from the man who avoids relationships, who's allergic to commitment?" Her voice held a skeptical tone.

"I deserve that." Fearing she might slip away, he kept a grip on her small hands. "You showed me how to care. I fell in love. I love you. I need you. You think I'm a heartbreaker, but I've always played fair. I've never before told a woman I loved her. Sometimes I can't breathe not knowing what to do about us. You are my love, my soul, my heart—*mi corazón.*"

She pushed to her feet and edged a little distance apart. "We're so different. I have my degree to finish, and you're being transferred."

"So you heard about that." He had to convince her. He wouldn't live the rest of his life without her. He couldn't. "I leave in a week."

"You like your exciting life, charging off in search of adventure. I need security."

"They don't transfer Group Supervisors nearly as much as other agents." Tension had his gut wound tight as a watch spring. He took a deep breath, tried to stop sounding like a bumbling idiot.

"What?"

"My promotion to GS came in. The SAC—the Special Agent in Charge—pushed for it. Guess he was grateful I cleared out the rotten apple. That carefree life of adventure, as you put it, isn't all it's hyped to be, Juliana. It's lonely. I'm finished with all that. I want love and family." Desperate to be closer, he tugged her between his legs.

"Well, congratulations then. I'm happy for you."

She stood rigidly, as if a hiking stick propped up her spine, but she didn't retreat. *Dios*, would this woman never surrender? "Where are they sending you?"

"Miami. One of the guys there is retiring. I'm going home. Don't make me go alone." He grinned, making sure his dimple winked at her. He needed all the ammunition he could muster. "It's thanks to you I can."

"Me? What did I do?"

"Your prodding helped me get past my *papá's* neglect and understand his fear of losing another son. You understand me. I need your wit and insight. I need *you*. Marry me."

She bent her forehead to his. "Oh, Rick, you've always been the man I wanted. I think I fell in love with you that day you slammed me to the floor in Jordan's apartment. I was afraid to trust you, but more afraid to trust myself."

"See what I mean? You're good for my ego. They say you can't go home again, but I can now with confidence. If you're with me. Go with me."

She leaned back, doubt crimping her forehead. "Right away?"

"It'd be hard. Your family, for instance." He ticked that obstacle off on his fingers.

She gave him a wry smile. "Now who's making a list?"

"Your family," he prompted with an unrepentant grin.

"Not a problem. Molly seems to have remembered, at least for the time being, that she's a mother. She and Jordan are two peas in a pod and can take care of each other."

"The SAC's in Jordan's corner. I doubt your

brother will do much jail time. He has too much to trade. I'll make sure you can come back for the trial. If there is one."

He held up his fingers again to tick off another obstacle. "College. You're in the middle of a semester."

A snort was her reply. "This semester is a wash. I missed too many assignments and classes. You must have a college or two in Miami." She grinned.

"So you'll do it? You'll come with me? And marry me?"

"Yes, *mi corazón.*" Her tongue tangled around the Spanish endearment. "My life here would be empty without you."

"Ah, you need me, you need my good humor, my charm, to keep you from being too serious, too—"

"Obsessive? Compulsive? And you need me to help you see the occasional down side of things."

"If we're together, down sides will be as rare as Antarctic butterflies."

She wrapped her arms around his neck and kissed him. He swept her up in a kiss of possession. Before he tore off her clothes and made love to her on this cold pile of rocks, he stopped and took her hand. "I'm staying at the Bar Harbor Inn. Come with me. I'll change, and we'll go out on that date we never had."

If she was feeling the way he did, if they went to his room, they wouldn't make it out on the town this time either.

Hooking her arms in her backpack, she sent him a languid look. "I'll race you down the trail."

*****

169

ABOUT THE AUTHOR

SUSAN VAUGHAN is the multi-published author of romantic suspense novels. Her books have won the Golden Leaf and More Than Magic awards and have been an *RT Book Reviews Magazine* Reviewer's Choice Nominee and a finalist for the Booksellers' Best and Daphne du Maurier awards. Her books have been translated into German, French, Spanish, and Icelandic and published in more than eleven countries. She's a West Virginia native, but she and her husband have lived in Maine for many years. Visit her at www.susanvaughan.com or "Friend" her on Facebook: Susan H. Vaughan. She loves to hear from readers: SHVaughan.author@gmail.com.

From Susan:
Thank you for reading *Never Surrender*. I hope you enjoyed it. If you did, please help others find the book by writing a short review at the retailer where you purchased it.

Continue for an excerpt from ONCE BURNED.

FROM ONCE BURNED

Lani Cameron parked her car in the Birch Brook Farm driveway. She put the house and attached small barn behind her and crossed the pasture. As she'd done twice a day since her arrival a week ago, she stopped at the splintered frame of the burned-out horse barn's doorway.

She turned her face to the late-afternoon June sun, absorbing brightness before lowering her gaze to the blackened remains. Not much left after twelve Maine winters. She bent to pick up a scrap of pine board. Her fingers clenched around the charred wood.

The remembered smell of creosote turned her stomach. If she closed her eyes she could feel the searing heat. Hear the roar. But she couldn't see more, couldn't see Gail's body, limp on the floor, couldn't— She dropped the wood as if it scorched her hand.

The sun shining through the structure's skeleton cast eerie shadows over the witch grass and daisies. Cow vetch twined its way up one of the posts. Green life amid the ashes—a mockery.

She needed to sell the farm, but without that phone call from Nora she might not have had the courage to return to Dragon Harbor to do it herself. When school had ended the second week of the month, she finished her students' final reports and booked it out of Concord. She prayed braving the scene of the fire would end her nightmares and help her remember, but the dreams were haunting her nightly, becoming more vivid. More real. The murderous fire monster, bigger and more frightening, woke her up in a cold sweat. She rubbed her arms in the sudden chill of memory.

Dammit, she would put up with a lack of sleep if her efforts led to answers.

She strode toward the farmhouse, seeking comfort in its white clapboards, peaked roof, and front door painted shut because everyone used the side-porch entrance to the kitchen. Repairs had to be done before the real estate agent would list the property.

As she reached the pasture's edge, a blue Jeep SUV pulled into the driveway and parked behind her car. A tall man in jeans and a faded University of Maine T-shirt emerged.

She held up a hand to shade her eyes from the sun and watched as he ambled toward her. Light-brown hair and strong boned features with bold planes and angles made her pulse flutter. He stopped a few feet from her and raised his gaze.

Her heart drummed, slamming against her ribs. *Jake Wescott.* The same blue eyes, but older, wiser, sadder. She'd expected to see her twin's old boyfriend, planned on it, but not yet. She'd wanted this first meeting on her own terms. Never mind. She would deal.

"What are you doing here?"

"I was just—" His mouth dropped open and he took a step back as if a horse had kicked him in the gut. "*Gail.*" Shaking his head, he blew out a breath. "Lani, is that you?"

Her throat closed. How long had it been since someone mistook her for her twin? A cruel joke,

172

except he wasn't joking.

The best defense is a good offense. She cocked a hip and flapped a hand at the scar on the left side of her face. "Who else would it be, Jake? Mrs. Frankenstein? And I repeat, what *are* you doing here?"

Tension crackled in the air between them. Her heart pounded like a kettledrum.

His face was a blank mask. Time had changed him. He was taller and broader shouldered. Lines etched into his cheeks added more than the three years he had on her. No familiar crooked grin, the one that used to melt every girl in Dragon Harbor. Including her. Although she'd kept it to herself. Back then he'd been open—funny and kind. But that wasn't the Jake here today. She didn't know this Jake with the unreadable, hard eyes.

"I'm living on my boat in the harbor while I take care of some family business. Fixing up Gram's house to sell it, for one."

Not what she meant but she'd get to that. "Nora told me you've been here since March. That you're in the FBI."

"Not FBI, ATF. Bureau of Alcohol, Tobacco, Firearms, and Explosives. I'm on leave. You mind me looking around in the horse barn, what's left of it?"

"No problem. Knock yourself out."

Permission received, if grudgingly, Jake strode toward the rectangular black scar stitched up by a few stubborn two by fours. He hadn't expected Lani to follow him but behind him, her sneakers swished through the grass, stirring up green smells of the freshly mown grass. If she noticed the awkward hitch in his stride, she said nothing.

She stopped at what was left of the barn doorway. He wondered if she *could* step inside, breaching some emotional barrier. She stood by stiffly, watching him meander through the charred wood.

"What are you doing? Looking for something?"

Not the first time he'd looked, but doubtful any clue to that horrible night would still be here. He kept hoping for insight. He kicked aside a board and bent, coming up with mangled metal. "A bicycle wheel. Yours or Gail's?"

"I don't know. Both of them could be in there. Gail called bike riding juvenile but I considered it healthy exercise. I rode to my job at Dragon Stables that summer. I still ride a bike." As if she couldn't bear to look anymore, she turned her back.

Seeing the wheel revived memories of that summer. The summer that had changed all their lives. His throat tightened. He couldn't bear to see this any more either.

He dropped the wheel and dusted off his hands as he joined her. "I'm surprised you came back. Seeing all this has to be doubly painful for you." He made a sweeping gesture.

As if considering her answer, she sighed and set out toward the house. The two of them walked silently away from the scorched relic of their past.

She turned to him, her eyes solemn and guarded. She was still smart-mouthed but not the light-hearted girl he'd once known. "Guess I thought it was time to face down my demons. The house is going up for sale. Granddad left the farm to me because of, well, you know. The caretaker kept the house in shape until he became too old. He died last year and I decided to sell. Porch needs shoring up, among other repairs. I'm doing some of the interior painting."

As they reached her car, she stopped him. "When I asked you earlier why you were here, I meant *here*, at Birch Brook Farm."

At the emotion in her voice, his throat tightened. "I need to know exactly what happened that night. Late to find much of a clue but I had to see what was left."

"Nora also told me you'd been reading up on the fire. You're investigating? Officially?"

He shook his head. "Nothing official. I've read over all the old news stories. That's all."

"If I'd gone out to the barn with her, if I'd seen the fire earlier..."

He knew all about survivor guilt. The beast clamped him in its jaws. If he hadn't left, Gail would still be alive. And a mottled white puckering wouldn't mar the skin of Lani's face. Other, more recent, images flashed through his mind, and pain jabbed him.

Forcing away the onslaught, he said, "Too many ifs. Neither of us can go back. A guilt trip gets you nowhere. No replay or do-over."

He drew in a breath, harnessing the emotions kicking around in his chest. Lani's perception had made him angry at himself because the elegant curve of her neck—identical to Gail's—and the pain in her eyes made him ache to touch her. No, the attraction was merely a flashback, a reaction to

Gail's lookalike. He'd hurt her, calling her by her twin's name. If he ran into her again, he'd be more thoughtful.

He didn't know how to deal with this new Lani. Twelve years ago, she hadn't tempted him. He'd been so blinded with lust for Gail. Teasing, seductive, partying Gail. He'd laughed with Lani, traded barbs with her, but hadn't known her well. The twins shared identical drop-dead gorgeous looks, but Gail and Lani had very different personalities.

And this Lani was different from that one. He couldn't have prepared for the change. Not the scarring, but the change in Lani the woman—hazel-gold eyes sharp enough to score glass. And her voice—low and smooth, like whiskey chased with honey. Sexy, even when she was skewering him.

Scars remained beneath the surface too, judging from the flashes of pain in her scorched-earth eyes. Defensiveness, and some bitterness, for damn sure. Who could blame her? The knowledge of what she'd suffered—still suffered—curled around the muscles of his chest and made it ache. He began edging toward his Cherokee.

She collected her keys, handbag, and a folder from the car's front seat. She slung the bag onto her shoulder and held up the folder, stuffed with papers. "After I got here, I decided I should read those news articles myself, the coverage I couldn't bring myself to look at back then. And I asked myself why a federal agent would check into a twelve-year-old tragic accident."

He opened his mouth to spout some inane answer but she held up a hand.

"Possibly this agent—who I now discover is an *arson* expert—suspects the accidental fire might have been something more. Am I warm? Hot?"

Her words seared him. "Lani—"

"Wait, there's more. I come home to find this expert digging for clues at the scene of the *accident*." Cheeks pink with emotion—temper or excitement, who knew—she charged onward. "Jake, if you suspect arson or some other foul play, I want in. I want to help, to *do* something. Gail was my twin, identical DNA. I need to *know*."

"The fire was declared an accident." Except what he'd read raised doubts of that as a fact. He wasn't ready to speak that aloud to anyone, especially to this woman. He made it two more steps down the driveway.

She huffed in disgust. "Remind me to invite you to my next Texas Hold'em game. I'll clean up."

"I have no information that indicates it *wasn't* an accident." The less he said about it, the better. Another few steps and he could escape before she could talk him into deputizing her.

"Official speak. Like that spokesman for the state police. 'We have no information at this time pending the investigation.' Bull crap." She jabbed a forefinger his direction. "You're the arson expert but I'm pretty good at research. I'll read the rest of these news clippings and go from there."

"Let me do the investigating. Stay out of this." Shit, he'd given away too much by warning her. "Okay, here's how you can help. Tell me what you saw that night."

Pain flashed in her eyes. "I would if I could. I can't tell you squat."

"But you must—"

"I must nothing! Ever since I woke up in that hospital bed, I've *tried* to remember. I thought coming back here, living in this house would bring it all back."

"But not yet, I take it."

She shook her head. Her mouth quirked up on one side. "So why do you want to shut me out? What's the risk in researching an *accident?*"

"Man, I'd forgotten what a hard bargain you drive. I'll share whatever I find with you."

"Good. Then we'll plan *our* next move." She beamed him a smile that rocked him back on the heels of his boat shoes. "Good to see you again, Jake. Don't be a stranger."

He said goodbye and hustled into his SUV. Watched her trot up the porch steps and swing through the door into the mud room. Sat staring at the closed door.

He shouldn't let her get involved even in a small way. Every time he saw her—saw Gail's face—would be another log on the burn in his gut. If someone had set the fire that killed Gail, the arsonist was a murderer and might do anything, *anything* to keep his crime secret. He wasn't worried for himself but he couldn't protect Lani. Not that she'd ask.

A scream from inside the house yanked him from the Jeep.

NEVER SURRENDER

CPSIA information can be obtained at www.ICGtesting.com
Printed in the USA
LVOW05s1529230414

382934LV00019B/1307/P